Haidji

Suicide Game

Cover design by Haidji.

www.haidji.blogspot.com

Selected songs, ringtones and soundtrack available in 2014.

Haidji

This book is dedicated to Raffaello

Haidji

Table of Contents

Haidji

Cast

Main Cast

The Council of Seven

White	The White Council member
Yellow	The Yellow Council member
Red	The Red Council member
Green	The Green Council member
Blue	The Blue Council member
Purple	The Purple Council member
Black	The Black Council member

Seven Candidates

Candidate 0907	Moma
Candidate 1518	Fabio Giovanni Cristiani
Candidate 3507	Anthony Henrik Gustav
Candidate 4914	Jens Plaato
Candidate 4918	Sarah Mondstein
Candidate 5151	Bianca White
Candidate 7195	The Scientist

Cast (in alphabetical order)

Albion

Alessandra

Alphabot

Anna

Calvin

Cassandra

Clare

Demir

Diana

John

Life in a Wire

Luca

Marcel Michaelsen

Marco

Metz Wurss

Michael

Morris

Philip

Steven Laurence

The Baby

The Betting agents

The Children's birthday party make-up artists

The dog

The Entrance woman - Elisabeth

The Food street vendors

The Geek

The Gravedigger

The Hare Krishna's

The Hostess

The Pharmacy guy

The Supermarket couple

The T-shirt vendors

Tim

Tom

Vincenzo Cristiani

And many others...

Original Music

Suicide Game

Lyrics - Gabriel Holtschlag

Music – Ralph Sahrmann

Suicide Freak

Lyrics - Ralph Sahrmann

Music – Ralph Sahrmann

A Kiss in Heaven

Lyrics – Haidji

Music – Ralph Sahrmann

Death on Death

Lyrics – Ralph Sahrmann

Music – Ralph Sahrmann

One Way Road

Lyrics – Haidji

Music – Haidji, Ralph Sahrmann

Haidji

A human life

Is the time that happens

while

The Earth takes a break

For you to live

between

Inhaling and exhaling your soul

from the un-endless space

Named infinity

Haidji

Introduction

Inside the Night Stadium it was almost dark, a kind of misty twilight atmosphere, no matter if day light or night-light.

It was the special effect that was the origin of the Stadium's name, created to allow special visual effects in every period of time, regardless of the season or weather conditions.

Created by one of the most important architects, Steven Laurence, it was the reason for his winning each of the Pritzker, Lubetkin and Global-Architecture prizes. Filtering and keeping part of the sunlight, inspired by micro resonator bottles, the Night Stadium was new, shining, intriguing and captivating, all at the same time.

Round and with capacity for 100,000 persons, the circular stadium had one main entrance, and of course, visible from inside of the first Stadium wall, all emergency doors were built. Once inside, there was a large Corridor all around the Stadium perimeter, with entrances to the Stadium's different sections and seating places. With small shops and spaces in the corridors for different purposes: the usual washrooms, personnel rooms, the Control room and the Council's Boardroom; the last two, with a view over the Stadium.

Special screens on the outside walls of the Stadium could make the Stadium turn into the colors around it, as would it be invisible sometimes; at other times, transparent, creating the impression for persons outside that it was possible to look inside through the Stadium's walls, as would they be watching, sitting inside.

Steven Laurence, also called The Architect, used laser and plasma projection technology to show outside the Stadium what was happening inside the Stadium, in larger than life, three-dimensional images.

The same projection technology was also deployed in certain places inside the Stadium, in front of seats and in the corridors; images floating in the air so people could see from every angle, inside and outside the Stadium, what the Council wanted people to see.

The Suicide Game was the Stadium's first official event.

Chapter 1

Step 1 – Day 1

A young girl was walking around inside the Stadium wearing a beautiful white dress, elegant in her Manolo shoes, carrying a baby in her arms, facing forward, and trying to cover its eyes with her hands while listening to a voice...

'The new game
The new mania
8000 candidates and
Only one will survive
Only one can win!
Live from the Night Stadium
Nothing compares to what you'll see here
Nothing compares to what you'll watch
See, choose your candidate, bet
Participate! It is ...
The new and unexpected... Suicide Game!

All that the girl, Alessandra, was thinking about was to get out of there, to walk quickly between the black shiny chairs into the dark corridors and disappear. She had entered the Stadium to apply for a job as one of the models, and she withdrew her application as soon as they explained to her exactly the Game's rules.

Alessandra was 20 years old; she was probably too old for the job, but she saw the announcement that they needed more models to work in the Game. She wasn't a model, but she looked like one, so she decided to try. She was happy as they called her and happy that she passed the initial casting a week ago, so she was there just to sign the contract and to start work on the same day.

But the Game rules made her feel terrified.

This...wasn't...a job... for her. For sure not.

Alessandra wanted to leave the space, but was hesitating for a moment, thinking about how to pay her bills, because she used up all her savings in the last months. Figuring out what to do now, with no money to pay her next rent; she was an optimist, she could feel, she felt she would find 'something', and she trusted her intuition.

She had thought this 'something' was the job in the Game, but it wasn't. Or maybe, in a certain and unexpected way, it was.

What she found, instead of a new job, came in front of her while she walked a little bit in circles, without finding her way out of the Stadium. It was a baby, crawling in front of her. 'Who brings a baby into a place like this?' she thought, while she took the baby in her arms to see if she could find the parents or someone responsible for it.

The baby smiled and embraced her.

Haidji

Nobody she asked was looking for a baby, and she saw only a man with a Red Cross uniform running in another direction.

With her high heels, Alessandra couldn't run after him, and he did not look nice anyway; she decided to keep walking around with the baby in her arms, to see if she could find the baby's parents.

Walking between the black seats in the already full Stadium, she could hear the Hostess of the Game and her words on her left side...on the right side, she could hear a religious group singing a Hare Krishna mantra in front of the Stadium. The Hostess's voice spilled over the boundaries of the Stadium and the Hare Krishna mantra seemed to be a bizarre kind of background music.

Alessandra noticed the Game was starting as she was still there, walking around the Stadium with a baby in her arms.

In the terror she felt, she surfaced the thought to protect the child she was carrying and to run away as soon as possible...out of there, and maybe try to find the baby's parents outside.

But it was a direct transmission of the Suicide Game, the cameras and monitors were already connected and turned on everywhere, so even if she didn't want it, she could hear the Hostess's voice everywhere, and see the live video images from the monitors.

The Stadium gates were already closed—no one could enter and no one could go out of there because the Game...the Game—had already started.

The gates had been closed to avoid the crowd in front of the Stadium invading it. There were no more places available inside the Stadium. People who couldn't buy a place to sit anymore were watching the Game on the big projections visible outside the Stadium. The automobile traffic had been rerouted. Only the food trucks had permission to enter and park at their rented spots at designated times. Deliveries to the Stadium and the minivans were also allowed, of course. People brought their chairs from home, sitting on the street as would they be in their living rooms, watching the Game on the projections outside and around the Stadium's walls.

There was nothing Alessandra could do to stop the Game, and there was no way to prevent it.

The Council had met, their decision had already been taken, the Game would begin in a few minutes and nothing she could do would avoid it. All she wanted, for now, was to bring the baby away from there, into a safe and quiet place. But, where was a quiet and safe place?

She passed through rows of chairs in the Stadium, listening to the mantra on the right and seeing the Hostess's images on her left.

The candidates in the Game, as a crowded mass of humanity, were being prepared; all with the same black clothes, bright black clothes, with a leather glove on their left hand, a glove attached to a line, a line of a new material. A new alloy material, very flexible and resistant. The glove was connected to the line that would bind them to life or death...the thin line.

The glove was also connected by an automatic docking system to a super-thin skin suit of Kevlar, invisible under their clothes.   The Kevlar skin suit cradled the pelvis and shoulder joints, so no joints could dislocate or bones break when they jumped. Bones were important and precious, no matter if they were alive or dead; better to not break any more than necessary.

John, one of the makeup artists, walked among the candidates, accompanied by Cassandra, who helped him with the makeup of those who were not yet prepared for the game.

Groups of two hundred candidates would jump together, one group after the other, for four days, day and night, until the first step of the game would finish; all eight thousand candidates would have a chance to be seen by anyone wanting to see the Game live and in person. Or maybe, everyone would see or hear about them anyway, given the media saturation.

And the first two hundred candidates were almost ready, waiting for the starting signal.

Ten groups each day, four in the morning, four after lunchtime and two in the evening, before the sunshine of the next day.

Cassandra was concentrating intensely and working hard to finish the makeup so they all could look great and gorgeous, because each one of them could be a winner...and she wanted to feel that she participated in their success. To be a part of it.

And she followed the rules: 'white faces, no expressions, the orange Game Symbol between the eyebrows, white lips'.

John was worried about the clothes and gloves, and was preoccupied looking at the hooks that attached the wires to the gloves of the candidates who were there for today's game. He saw the t-shirts, belts and pants, socks and shoes, gloves and lines, all in black except for the makeup, white face with the orange Symbol and white lips, as would they have made a new image from the traditional street pantomime artist's image.

The Stadium was round and so was the stage, which was a platform that came from the center that was like an open elevator that could elevate up to fifty-five meters over the ground floor.

The candidate's jumps would be from a height of fifty meters above the ground, the same height as the principal rows of chairs, the most expensive seats in the house.

The wire length was about twenty meters, and the Stadium crew was already prepared with their cameras and reporters. Even the welcome cocktails for the survivors were ready, inside a corridor on the ground level, waiting with the models to be placed on the platform, to be seen by the crowd and then given to the survivors, all part of the spectacle.

Looking down to the ground of the Stadium and to the elevators that also brought the minivans and candidates to the ground, Cassandra felt dizzy. She saw the platform on the ground of the Stadium, fifty meters below the principal row of chairs, as would there be a precipice in the middle of the Stadium. She tried to concentrate on her job; it was probably good that the make up teams worked in rooms on the street level. Cassandra tried hard to be focused in her work. After finishing, she could go home and watch it all on the TV, and probably she would see more than what she could see there live, because she was working and could not really see or appreciate all that what was happening around her.

She was part of the first makeup artists' team. It was an honor for her to prepare the first candidates of the Game. There was not much time, she could spend only a few minutes with each person, and they all needed to look alike; there was lots of work to do and only a short time before the official start was to begin.

The first group was almost ready and after the second group, there would be a ten-minute break and then two more groups jumping before lunchtime. But in this situation, lunchtime was no time for a real meal, and she was already starving.

Two hundred persons dressed the same way, and ten makeup artists, divided into five different teams, all with the same outfits, just in non-shiny clothes, as if they were all kids or clones coming out of the same laboratory, all sharing a deep desire...the desire to win at any cost.

G

The Hare Krishna mantra continued, even though no one had said they were hired to be there to perform, but they appeared, and maybe it seemed they had been hired for the event, because their voices and orange clothes seemed to naturally become part of the environment.

It did not seem odd that they did not have their usual money donation cups in their hands, or Hare Krishna books to sell along with incense; those things would seem to be at the wrong place, at the wrong time, because it seemed no one would want to buy them.

And finally, and almost unexpectedly, a few minutes before the start, the first group was ready. Going down the elevators, they had a last check of their gloves inside a room on the ground floor. Coming out of the corridors on the ground floor, they walked through the sand ground onto the round platform, in the middle of the Stadium, where each candidate tied the hook of his or her own wire into a metal ring on the edge of the platform, showing once again their own free will about their decision to be part of the Game, but with impassive faces, as if showing their ambition would have cut their souls, demolishing their own free will.

From above, for the audience they looked like black ants coming from different directions walking to the round platform. But everywhere there were screens and projections, showing them up close and in detail, while the platform was rising from the ground to the height of fifty meters. All of the persons in the principal row of seats, at the fifty meters' height, were already seated.

Accompanied by the voice of the pretty Hostess, and while the security personnel, also wearing the same clothes as the rest of the staff, adjusted the ropes, gloves and candidates, the time counter started at 50, matching the jumping height in meters of the platform.

The counter started to show on the projections inside and outside the Stadium, showing the number 50 and going down second after second. 49...48...47...46...45...

With her Alexander McQueen Shoes and Dolce&Gabbana 'Femme Fatale' red dress, green eyes and long brown hair, she was almost floating over the platform coming up from the Stadium's ground. Waking up deeply grooved fantasies in the male and female public's minds, the Hostess walked in silence for a few seconds, as would she be coming out of their dreams.

As the platform stopped, she announced the game:

'Now, live from the Night Stadium, especially for you,

SUICIDE GAME!

The new game
The new mania
8000 candidates and
Only one will survive
Only one can win!

Live from the Night Stadium
Nothing compares to what you'll see here
Nothing compares to what you'll watch
You have already chosen your candidate,

You have Made your bet

To be part of a

New and unexpected game

Now it's time to let all be in the laps of the gods

And when the bell rings...it is time to jump for your life!

She spoke, as would she be the human part of the counter's voice, as the counter displayed its numbers on all screens inside and outside the Stadium, inside people's homes, and on their hands in mobile phones or other devices.

10...9...8...7...6...5...4...3...2...1!

And the jump bell rang out loudly

JUMP!

And the candidates jumped, all at the same time, still hearing the echo of the bell's sounding, as the Hare Krishna mantra started again.

In their homes, in front of the TV, holding their mobile devices, and even in the Stadium, people jumped, standing up, caught in the adrenaline rush of the moment, as the bell rang out.

Free falling bodies. After a twenty meter free fall, some wires broke, and the bodies continued down, falling on the Stadium ground, where dumb screams where muffled by the sound of the Hare Krishna mantra.

Haidji

Outside the Stadium and also inside, everyone saw the candidates jumping and falling, even though some persons sitting very high up the Stadium did not have a good view. The 3D laser and plasma screen images were captivating, so people would concentrate on the candidates jumping; nobody saw or noticed the dead bodies on the Stadium ground, or really even thought about them.

Quickly came the ushers, all dressed in gray—the same color of the sand on the Stadium ground floor, with their minivans. Some removed the bodies, counted them, and took note of the numbers written inside their gloves, and brought them into different minivans to bring them to the elevators, to reach the street level floor and the right department, already separated by age and gender.

Others were busy spreading new sand on the floor, sweeping it over the places of impact, and taking out the remains of fresh blood with a shovel.

Each candidate had signed a complete donation form at the time of their registration in the game, so their bodies and belongings would never be claimed by their loved ones.

Meanwhile...the survivors were swinging on their lines, thirty meters from the ground, catching the attention of all the other persons present or watching on the media. They had been trained to never look down, and to smile and wink. Most of them managed only a pale smile, having survived deep inside a mad frenzy.

The cameras showed them smiling to the cameras, while the platform was now moving down to the ground, where young models dressed in blue, the color of the sky, were waiting on the ground to walk onto the platform with tables filled with transparent champagne glasses, to celebrate their victory.

125 glasses.
125...was the number, while the others who had jumped were already being forgotten.

As the platform touched the ground, the winners walked onto it again and the models rolled the tables onto it.

Then the platform moved up slowly again and stood at the height of the principal row of chairs, for the ten minutes of celebration, while the next group was being prepared to jump. The cameras kept moving between the first survivors, and the next group of candidates, never showing the ground of the Stadium or the already dead candidates.

After the celebration, the platform moved down, the winners winking to the audience and getting ready to leave the platform to enter the same minivans used by the ushers some minutes before. Elevators would take them to the street floor and they would leave the Stadium.

Haidji

They would return to the condominium that was nearby, a big modern construction made with concrete and green glass, a kind of modern ghetto like modern fancy condominiums used to be, because human beings like transparency in their neighbors' lives, while they figure out how to protect their own privacy. Inside the condominium all was virtually transparent, while the guards on the security gated entrance and some glass shards and electric wires over the walls could protect them from the dangerous outside world.

With the transparency and some cameras in the right places, the Council knew almost everything that happened inside the condominium. They knew where each of the candidates was staying.

After surviving the first step, the survivors would move into new rooms, the rooms for Step 2 of the Game, while the belongings of those who would never return were donated (or even better, sold) to certain kinds of 'charities', as the candidates had also signed in their registration waivers a clause that they would donate everything in their bodies, and left in their condominium rooms, to the administrators of the Game.

Meanwhile, the second group of candidates entered the Game and took their places on the platform while persons dressed in yellow walked among the crowds of spectators to sell betting tickets, while other groups of persons dressed in red were walking, selling drinks and meat sandwiches. Betting huts had been built, but in a hurry, so there weren't enough to attend to all the spectators, or even the players, some of whom also placed bets before they were to make their jumps.

The voice of the beautiful Hostess rose again over the murmur of the crowd:

'Wow, that was exciting! The first jump of the Game has already happened, did you make your bet? Do you already have your candidate? Soon it is time for the second group to jump. Here they are! Let's welcome them all with a big round of applause!'

And there they were, the second group of candidates, standing on the edge of the platform, hearing the Hostess' voice while the counter started...

'SUICIDE GAME!

The new game
The new mania
8000 candidates and
Only one will survive
Only one can win!
Live from the Night Stadium
Nothing compares to what you'll see here
Nothing compares to what you'll watch
You have already chosen your candidate,

You have Made your bet

To be part of a

New and unexpected game

Now it's time to leave it all in the laps of the gods

And when the bell rings...it is time to jump...for your life!

10...9...8...7...6...5...4...3...2...1!

JUMP!'

The crowd jumped up again in their seats, and backwards, while the candidates were falling down through the air.

'What a game! What a day!' announced a commentator on the TV. 'You have never seen anything like that!'

The second group's jump left ninety survivors, the third group's eighty-five, the fourth one hundred and thirty, the fifth—to many people's surprise, 192. There were 105 survivors in the sixth jump; the seventh, 108; 85 in the eighth; and in the ninth and tenth jumps, 106 and 96 respectively. Interesting numbers, and there was also betting on these numbers, not just betting on the identities of the jumpers, but on the number of survivors, so there was a lot of work for the odds-makers.

And while a seemingly increasing number of people walked among the crowd, dressed in yellow to sell betting tickets for today, the crowd was already running to the betting stands to buy some tickets for the next day.

6

From the initial 2000 candidates who jumped in step one of the Game, only 1122 remained alive.

They were waiting to participate in the second step, taking part in seminars at the condominium, where they were fully moved in; as though they believed this was their new home and they would live there until the end of the Game, and emerge as the lone survivor.

For now, at least, post-game interviews at the condominium were prohibited, but everyone, including the odds-makers, wanted to know why these people had moved in, like they were moving into a new home. There was considerable gossip, and some serious discussion, about what this meant, if anything, about the odds and who would win the game.

And then the Hostess, wearing the Femme Fatale red dress, as would she be the one that decided over life and death in the Game, slid over the platform that was descending to the ground floor. She was laughing and proclaiming the results after the 10 jumps on the first day, and the success of the first day. She promised more excitement and adventure in the Game between life and death, now coming up for the second game day with 2000 fresh new candidates, while the Stadium lights were fading away...and the yellow dressed bet sellers and red dressed food sellers counted how many bitcoins profit they had made on their first day.

White, Yellow, Red, Blue, Green, Purple and Black entered the conference room in silence. Alphabot from Alpha Smart Systems, the robot created by Vladimir Belyy, opened the door for them and then left the room to take care of his other obligations. It was Steven Laurence's newest acquisition, his Personal Assistant to help here and there, wherever he needed a hand in the Stadium events.

Wearing colored togas according to their names, White, Yellow, Red, Blue, Green, Purple and Black took their fixed places around the round conference table, sitting down one after another, in a clockwise direction. Each of their respective parts of the round table lit up, in their respective color, when they spoke; voice recognition software also ensured they were always in their own places.

In front of each member was a polished metal sphere, about 3cm in diameter, which could be opened in two equal parts. The sphere was part of the voting system. Inside the sphere was a button that changed the color inside into red or green, by pressing it; red was for disapproval and green for approval. But the light would come on only after closing and then opening the sphere again, to maintain the privacy of the system.

A cup with coffee was already there for each one of them, in front of their places.

In the middle of the table rested a crystal ball, part of the voting system.

They were all of the Council Members, the ones who decided all that happens in the Game.

For about one hour they had their meeting about the first day and they voted on different issues for the next days. From outside their room, sometimes workers walking in the corridor could hear the sound of metal rolling, and crystal.

By request, Alphabot came back to open the door.

They stood up from their places, one after another, in a counterclockwise direction. In the reverse order from which they entered, and more or less satisfied with the voting results and with the first day of this first step, Black, Purple, Green, Blue, Red, Yellow and White left the conference room.

Alphabot removed the coffee cups from the table. One member did not drink his coffee. Alphabot closed the conference room's door.

Council Table

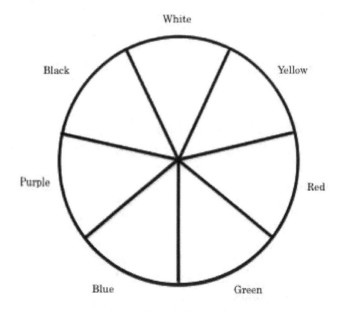

Haidji

Chapter 2

Candidate 0907: Moma

His nick or code name was Moma; his real name?

He probably did not remember his own name in the middle of so many fake passports and IDs; Mohamed something. His family moved into a new country, but kept their roots. Cultural roots, his father used to say, we need to keep them. They make our country essence alive, no matter where we are. Our country is inside ourselves and we carry and expand it to the places where we go and live. Our country is the skin of our soul; it is the color of our Flag that makes us who we are, we can live without a country, our home is inside of us, it is what we carry with us; wherever we go.

Moma was the fifth of seven kids, praying many times a day every day, and having to read the same books again and again in his free time. The first book he remembered reading was 'Milestones'.

And he never forgot some quotes from the book. Such as:

'Mankind is on the brink of a precipice...it is essential to have a new leadership'.

And every time he started to read again he almost fell asleep by the words, repeating like a mantra, the same meaning in other words.

His mind woke up one day reading: '...peoples of any race or color—Arabs, Romans or Persians—are equal under the banner of God'; this was all he could keep, apart from 'no sovereignty except God's, no law except from God'.

Growing up in Europe, his beliefs mixed up: God was love, all persons are equal; and so, God's law should be what his heart tells him to do.

The rest of the book passed by in his soul like a too soft wind on a too hot day; he did not keep the words or even feel them. Like raindrops over fire they evaporated away from him, without touching or coming close to his heart or mind.

Moma had been in a special terrorist camp. He had previously obtained his Ph.D. in Explosives Engineering from the University of Missouri, which had the best professors of destruction. He learned to be in silence and do his work quietly. Moma learned to be almost invisible, not too much the party guy, not too much a nerd. A common guy that is always there but no one notices. A specialist in bombing attacks, he knew how to build bombs, but his special skill was how to disarm them without being noticed or even leaving a mark.

He was there…in every big attack, in every big event; but what his friends and colleagues did not know about him was that for each bomb that exploded, seven others were disarmed or failed; they thought that maybe the dealer sold them bad products, or an infiltrated agent had been there, or just bad luck happened, and they searched exhaustively between foreigners for spies, for CIA or FBI agents.

But the seed for failure was inside the main group already…so quiet he was, so cooperative he seemed to be…Moma never forgot the words engraved in his heart from the first time he read them: 'All peoples are equal….' So for each bomb that exploded in each attack in which he was involved, he disarmed seven others.

A long time ago he decided to be what they wanted him to be, a terrorist, and a good one. Moma decided also to follow his heart and be a good terrorist and never kill someone. Instead of killing, he saved lives. He decided to be a good terrorist, with his own point of view.

Years ago, Moma was involved in an attack.

Moma knew that something, like a sign coming from the sky, would happen in the middle of the city to distract people's attention and then, around every 15 minutes thereafter, a bomb would explode.

He did not know exactly what would happen, because it wasn't the group he usually worked with that prepared this attack, and because of the fear of FBI and CIA spies, all was more secret than usual. He tried to discover the details but failed, all he knew was that would be something big.

A kind of signal coming from the sky to start, and then activation of all the other bombs around the city. One Bomb, every 15 minutes.

Moma looked again at the New York City map trying to figure out where the attack would start; maybe he could disarm these bombs too?

Depending on where the attack started, the bomb closest to it would explode first, with the other bombs following in a similar direction.

All he could do was wait for the signal and then run to the closest bomb to the signal site, to deactivate it.

He couldn't deactivate the bombs before the attack, because there would be guards around it until the signal came. Only then they would leave their spots, not to be caught.

He looked at the American credit card he had pick-pocketed from some teenager at Times Square, too full of beer or tequila to even notice, eyes bulging at the neon marquees boasting topless and nude live stage shows. When the kid sobers up, he thought, he and his friends will notice, and it will be a big tragedy for them.

How little would they understand the role their minor tragedy would play in the secret history of the City? He smiled to himself; this cesspool of American filth, so detested by his terrorist clansmen, had in fact provided him with some essential tools he would use to save the City. Only in America. In America, the land of opportunity.

He used the credit card to buy burner phones, one from each of the City's mobile phone networks; phones he needed to deactivate the bombs. He still needed to discover to which networks they were connected. So, he needed all them. He bought the phones from the networks' kiosks, in locations unlikely to have surveillance cameras. AT&T, Sprint, T-Mobile, Verizon Wireless. He thought about the pandemonium that would probably follow after the signal came, better to already have the phones ready to use.

He then set about to chart his route.

The most efficient way to reach his seven targets before the bombs could explode. He figured out different ways, depending on the first signal.

Moma knew the City pretty well, but couldn't predict what would happen when the first signal would come. It was foreseeable that the City's transportation systems could break down or become gridlocked when all hell broke loose, so he devised several alternate routes, still not knowing what was the start signal. Each route would take him to the targets.

With the routes done, he was ready to practice them, and then he would just wait for the start, still trying to figure out how to be able to avoid any problems along the way.

The first plane hit at 8:46am.

New York, New York. Manhattan.

Moma was sitting outside a café in the financial district, this most pristine of September mornings. He now knew the code: 'first attack' is the signal; it means all seven bombs are now armed, set to detonate in 15-minute intervals. A septuplet of falling dominoes of blood and body parts. Added to the couplet of destruction and death they told him would start the carnage that morning, made nine. Nine for New York. That day. Nine eleven.

American Airlines Flight 11 hit the North Tower at 8:46. Moma heard the boom. They hadn't told him the signal would be an attack on the Twin Towers. Only that the signal would be an attack somewhere in the northwestern part of the financial district. And there would be a second signal, which would either confirm the first signal, or be a backup, in case there was a failure with the first signal. In the same area. So, he had picked a café in the southeastern part.

His mind raced through the alternate routes he had planned earlier; game theory now being put into action. He looked at his watch. It was now 8:49.

Moma had less than 12 minutes to reach and disarm the first bomb.

He needed to get to 225 Liberty Street. Quickly. Headquarters of Merrill Lynch Wealth Management. Virtually across the street from the Twin Towers.

First responders would probably soon be swarming the World Financial Center, maybe even setting up a perimeter or something. He kick-started his black motorcycle and sped off. He reached the underground parking, pulled the ticket from the entry control, and found the large white van. To disarm the bomb he needed one of the four cell phones, he needed to find out which one to use; it was the third one. It was now 9:00am. He tore up the exit ramps. The exit gate was open.

Everyone was standing outside, looking up at the skyline, a skyline that was now on fire. He had disarmed the first bomb.

His next stop was the New York Stock Exchange. Second bomb. He pointed his motorcycle south on West Street and gunned it. He heard what sounded like the roar of an airplane, but it was hard to tell with the noise of his motorcycle and helmet.

But there was no doubt about the sound, when United Airlines Flight 175 flew into the South Tower at 9:03. That was signal number two; he knew it. He had about 10 minutes to disarm the bomb at the NYSE. He made it, using phone number two.

Now he had to get to the Federal Reserve, at Liberty Place. Bomb number three. After that, he had to go uptown, much longer distances. He had to make up some time. Instead of taking the usual route taken by taxis from the NYSE to Liberty Place, he just rode down the pedestrian walkway on Nassau Street, reaching the Federal Reserve in less than two minutes. Nobody even turned an eye to him.

Everyone was watching the Twin Towers on fire.

He wasn't sure if Bomb number three was tied to phone number one or number four, because the signal types were similar; he needed more time to figure it out.

Working calmly and efficiently, he was relieved, as his conclusion was correct; it was phone number four, and bomb three was disarmed.

Now he had to get to the Stern School of Business at New York University, near Washington Square South. He calculated this would take about 10 or 12 minutes under normal conditions, in a car. If traffic wasn't already becoming gridlocked, or blocked by first responders, he figured he could do better than that on his bike. Police wouldn't be worried about stopping a motorcyclist who was speeding a little bit, especially one going in the opposite direction to their attention. They would all be looking up, downtown at the financial district skyline, not at him going uptown on Sixth Avenue.

He made it in 8 minutes. Found the fourth bomb. Disarmed it. Plenty of time to spare, using phone number one.

From NYU, he had to get to Grand Central Station. Again, about 10 minutes under normal conditions. Sixth Avenue would do the trick; closer to West 42nd Avenue he could always hop over to Madison, Park or Lexington, depending on conditions. He made good time. He disarmed the fifth bomb with phone number three. He was especially pleased about his success at Grand Central Station.

Now he had some extra time in the bank.

The last bombs were in posh sections of midtown Manhattan, so he was glad to have the extra time, just in case. You never knew how midtown Manhattanites would react when they saw the Twin Towers on fire.

Next stop. Trump Tower. Fifth Avenue. Between 57th and 56th. About 15 blocks give or take. 5 minutes for that one, then onto the next; things were going well, it would be easy.

Not so easy.

Having disarmed bomb number six with phone number four, he made his way out of Trump Tower. He preferred handmade and special jewelry with soul to mass-produced superficial fashion-hip products. Exiting Trump Tower through the retail level, he thought for a brief moment that if the world would be perfect, then Tiffany's and the Trump Organization should find a way to recognize his good deeds by selling real, special things in their stores, instead of boxes of emptiness and marketing illusions.

One more stop. Bomb number seven.

He thought about how to best reach it. The bomb was located on the ground floor of the Metropolitan Museum of Art. In the Nolen Library. The bomb was placed in the collection of books on digital art.

He could get to the Library very quickly from the Museum's underground parking lot; alternatively, he could use the Plaza entrance at 81st Street.

Either route got him in on the ground floor.

It would take him eight or ten minutes in regular traffic, depending on whether he took Madison or Park Avenue; but maybe longer now, given the pandemonium he was starting to see on the streets. Police, ambulances, all sorts of emergency traffic heading south; taxis and cars heading north or east.

What about another route?

Through or around Central Park? It would be maybe 15 minutes if he took Central Park West and then doubled back to the Museum via the West 85th Street Transverse. But if he went that way, he could dip into the Park if necessary and ride the Park roads, maybe less risk of traffic snarls, and he could even ride his motorcycle on the grass if necessary. Surely by now anyone in Central Park would be thinking of nothing other than their SMS texts and email messages, or figuring out how to help people, or searching for friends and survivors, or trying to understand why New York was on fire. He opted for Central Park West, and would pick his route through or around the Park, on the fly.

Turning onto Central Park West, an ambulance heading south, driving in the middle of the road, crossed his path in the middle of the intersection.

Hitting the brakes hard, his rear wheel locked up and he fell underneath his bike as it skidded across the road, giving him an instant case of painful road rash and, he thought for a moment, maybe a broken elbow. Worse, all his phones had spilled across the street and a car had run over one of them, but he had not yet noticed this.

Covered in his own blood, he picked up the phones and jumped back on his bike, racing off to arrive in time at the last bomb.

This was supposed to be an easier one, the last bomb. But he was now behind, by 3 minutes at least. He arrived at the last bomb less than 5 minutes before its stipulated explosion time, full of pain, and covered with blood.

It was then he noticed that a phone was missing...and it was exactly the one he needed to disarm this bomb.

Without the phone, he needed to go back to old methods. He made his disarming work by hand, feeling as American as MacGyver or apple pie. He did it...even without having any chewing gum.

So, in less than 120 minutes, Moma had done his work; quietly, in his silent way, he had saved the city from another unbelievable and possibly even bigger catastrophe.

He had made sure that all seven bombs were disarmed.

Now, years later, a new attack was planned for a Stadium, where a game would be, a game with a huge public attendance. With over 100,000 people inside. And probably the same amount, or even more, outside.

And Moma was the one chosen by the terrorist group, because he was a specialist; he was the one that would press the command button to explode all seven bombs inside the Stadium. And he was also the one that should create the bombs. Maybe the group had started to find it strange that so many bombs were not working well, all these years, so they decided to have their own specialist, himself, taking care of it.

The attack should occur on one of the last game days.

And Moma, to be able to do his work, needed to be in the middle of the Stadium, so there would be no interference with the signals to the bombs. This was a suggestion made by Moma himself; to ensure that he would not fail in this attack, he should be a candidate and take part in the Game.

A large amount of money would transfer to a Council member, the Yellow one, so that Moma could enter the game.

With the guarantee that Moma would survive until the last game day, the terrorist group made a plan to also have some of their members inside the Stadium, watching the game from day one, as part of the crowd, until the final day.

Yellow did not ask the reason for Moma's entry into the game and the requested guarantee; for him it was just one candidate more between zero and 8000, who probably wouldn't win anyway. And sure as sure was, Yellow was also very sure that he could keep Moma alive until the last game day.

One candidate more in the game—and some digits changing in his secret bank account. Yellow was ok with that.

The terrorist group also asked for a personal trainer for Moma, for some extra lessons, to help with the neuro-linguistic programing (NLP) seminars. Of course, the trainer would also receive an extra reward, to make some special exercises with him before the last game day.

Moma's assignment: 'Seven bombs for seven Brothers'.

He knew the attack was to be inside the Stadium. He was told the date; it was to be the in one of the last days of the Game, when the Stadium was packed full and the whole world would be watching live and on TV and on every portable or fixed electronic device.

He was told the planned outcome: the complete obliteration of the Stadium and everything around it, preferably up to a one-block radius. They left the choice of the explosive technology, and the placement of the seven terrorists inside the Stadium. All up to him. He was the Specialist.

That one variable—the technology plan, left to him—gave him the opening he needed.

Nobody would or could check his handiwork; there were no 'quality control' men in white lab coats.

His idea was simple. Inspired by a chameleon. A chameleon that changed its guts on the inside, not its colors on the outside.

The bomb vests would need to be compact and made of materials that would not trigger any of the security devices at the Stadium. What was needed was more like a super-thin Kevlar body armor vest, not the clunky vest style preferred in the Middle East, which could be easily hidden under loose robes. There was no way the seven terrorist bomb carriers would attempt to open the vests to look at their guts or otherwise tamper with them.

They knew the protocol: tamper with a suicide bomb in a vest, in any way, and it detonates immediately.

What the NLP trainer, Yellow, the other Council members and the terrorist group did not know was that some things were already engraved with the fire of admiration deep inside of Moma's mind. So deeply, that not even a seminar with the best NLP guru could erase or replace them.

Moma was a terrorist. He created the seven bombs for seven brothers. But he was a good terrorist; for him, '...peoples of any race or color—Arabs, Romans or Persians—are equal under the banner of God'. That was his programming.

He created a vest for himself, too.

Chapter 3

Step 1 – Day 2

Cassandra woke up feeling...different.

She fell asleep with the window open, and the smell of flowers had invaded the room, taking part in her dreams.

She lived in a modern building, in the new part of town, and had never realized that there was a park on the other side of the street, because she was always late to go out to work; almost always before sunrise, and she would normally return after sundown.

While closing the window, she saw the park between the buildings and sighed, thinking about maybe going there someday for a walk. Since she moved into this neighborhood, her outgoings were summarized by quick purchases in a small supermarket around the corner, where, she noticed, worked a nice couple; or to watch movies in the local cinema, or spend some time in pubs with some of her friends or colleagues.

She closed the window, but the flowery perfume smell was already inside, filling the entire room; but she did not notice, she was already very late, and she needed to rush.

The game was going live again this morning and she couldn't be late; her work was too important, and John, her colleague, would not like to do it all alone.

As she arrived, the crowd was already in front of the Stadium; many had spent the night there, sleeping in front of the Entrance, in sleeping bags, or tents, so as not to miss their preferred places on the second day. Given the strong interest in the Game, there were already some groups selling both fake and real tickets, online and on the streets close to the Stadium.

She went through the crowd and showed the electronic bracelet that allowed her to access the Stadium before the public was allowed to enter. She should use it, all the time, for the complete event: each person that belonged to the game staff wore one. She remembered hearing that each person in the public will also wear one, and each candidate also, with different programming.

John was already stressed, looking at the clock. The candidates were already being prepared and Cassandra had not yet arrived.

It was the second game day, and he was working on the second group of this day: 200 persons in each group, 5 makeup artists teams; so he and Cassandra had 40 candidates, meaning 20 candidates for each to take care of...and she was late.

John was already working on the candidates, hard and necessarily fast work; and they could spend only a few minutes with each person, so where could Cassandra be? She was professional, in all the projects they had worked together in the past, she never came late, she was more like someone who arrives 5 minutes before work starts and creates a good mood around her.

She came in running, her red hair like a flame flying around her head. John was relieved, he didn't want to fall behind the other makeup artists, it was hard to get good work at this time in the economy, and a silent and invisible competition seemed to be there among the makeup artists; sometimes some work material was broken or disappeared suddenly, so as to delay things or cause him to be flustered...it wasn't a good thing for his career.

Cassandra tied her hair together and was already wearing her work uniform, all black, which from a distance made it difficult for someone to distinguish the makeup artists from candidates; the only difference was that while the candidates' clothes were shiny, the staff used a matte version of the same clothes, with no white makeup or game symbol on their forehead.

She was working quickly, already on the second group, now on a candidate's face, as a red hair lock passed in front of her eyes.

Her hair wasn't tied right, so she blinked her eyes, moved her head... and then she saw his blue eyes, while he moved his arm and head in an instantaneous reflex to take her hair away from his own face.

Their hands touched, because she had the same reflex.

It was just for a half second, and after that, he was again the same apathetic figure, like all other candidates, a kind of statue that didn't have expressions and didn't show feelings or intentions. But time had stopped, for this half second, and there was a feeling, and intention, without him showing it right away.

For this half second, he had woken up from his apathetic state and looked into her eyes.

He was candidate number 2252, there to be jumping in the second group, on this second game day.

Cassandra noticed that he had a scar on the left side of his face, and against all rules, instead of covering the mark, she accentuated it; she didn't want him to be like all the others there, she wanted him to be special, different.

Cassandra thought she had found her candidate, the one she wanted to win the game, but the truth was that she had found something else, something she had and lost some times in her past, and never expected to find again.

Haidji

Although she could not grasp the thought consciously, it felt as though she had found something elusive. Love, perhaps? Even though she could not think it, she could feel it.

And then she moved to the next candidate, against her own will, because John was already complaining that she had spent too much time in preparing this guy, asking her, did she have had a bad night? She already came to work late, so, what did she want to achieve by delaying her work also? Still sleeping, still dreaming around?

'Cassandra, we have work to do here, we can rest and dream at lunchtime, and try to find out why our work materials sometimes disappear...'

But, fortunately for Cassandra, John was busy grumbling and being cranky, looking for his makeup instruments, he couldn't find all of them again...it was good that he always had some extra ones in his bag, and that he had not noticed the scar on the guy's face, the mark.

G

The game started, and the live transmission continued, but on that day, Cassandra didn't want to see it live; only at home, on the TV.

She accompanied the candidate with the mark and closed her eyes, as he disappeared into the group that was to jump next.

The group went down with the elevators and entered the game platform.

Standing on the edge of the platform, fifty meters over the Stadium ground, they looked like all the same. But Cassandra could see the scar in her chosen candidate face.

The Hostess announced the next jump, and after a few words, the countdown would start:

'The first group of the day has celebrated already; now, we have the second group of the day. Two hundred candidates more, here, ready to jump for you! What an amazing day! I thank every one of you, here, at home; at work watching on your mobile devices, in front of the Stadium, walking on the street...wherever you are, you are here with me! Welcome to the second jump of this second day!

We are all together here in...

SUICIDE GAME!

The new game
The new mania
8000 candidates and
Only one will survive
Only one can win!

Live from the Night Stadium
Nothing compares to what you'll see here
Nothing compares to what you'll watch
You have already chosen your candidate,

You have Made your bet

To be part of a

New and unexpected game

Now it's time to leave it all in the laps of the gods

And when the bell rings... it is time to jump...for your life!

10...9...8...7...6...5...4...3...2...1!

JUMP!'

And the second group of candidates jumped.

Cassandra held her breath, while her heart was beating faster, as he jumped, opening her eyes only when it ended, to see that he was among the survivors. She tried to calm down and breath deeply, and normally, again.

Her candidate survived, Cassandra, relieved, tried to concentrate again on the next group of candidates.

The day passed by fast. And the other groups entered the game, accompanied by the Hostess' voice; the public was blown away with the game's adrenaline. And went out of the Stadium during the breaks, to breath or maybe search for a certain kind of street food they couldn't find inside. There were so many food trucks outside.

The bets had increased a lot after the first game day and at the end of the day, only 920 candidates remained from the initial 2000; only 920 survivors from the 2000 candidates who jumped on this second game day. So it was almost a miracle that Cassandra's chosen candidate survived.

As the Hostess, sliding over the platform with her Alexander McQueen shoes, announced the end of the second game day, promising an unforgettable third game day, without forgetting to mention that the public could buy and wear t-shirts with the game symbol to support the Game and the candidates, Cassandra was thinking about 2252.

Cassandra was happy and sad at the same time: happy because 2252 survived, and sad too; now, she would see him again, perhaps; but only in the next step of the game.

She did not know much about him...so she began to wonder and imagine things about him, his life story, why did he seem to look at her in that half-second, why was he in the game, why had their paths crossed at all...?

Haidji

There was nothing else better for her to do than to engage in this musing, to make her workday time pass by faster. Or, was she really just trying to make the workday time pass by faster? Was there more to this than musing? She had a conscious thought that musing about something like this elusive feeling was, perhaps, not like musing about something she could remember, at all. Or maybe it was a new feeling, or maybe it was something she had read about in a good literary work, or seen in a classic film, so her dim memory of an elusive feeling was not a memory of a real event, but of a fiction.

Haidji

Chapter 4

Candidate 1518 – Fabio

Black hair, black eyes, gentleman, passionate; a common Italian man.

His name was Fabio Giovanni Cristiani. As a child Fabio used to spend the afternoons and weekends in his grandfather's company, riding his first bike, made especially for him. In exactly the right size. He already had a road bike made for him by measure, while his friends were still learning to use the tricycle, and while others were learning the numbers, he already knew them and was learning the name of the 'Giro d'Italia' winners for the last...10 years.

'Nonno' Vincenzo was a master bike frame builder in Italy. An original. One of the true founders and masters of the trade. Fabio remembered many hot summer days and weeks during school vacations, spent in his grandfather's shop near Milano, watching grandfather and his crew work. In typical Italian fashion, the sounds of their work—loud noises from cutting and rolling special metal alloys—were most often completely buried under the din of the workers' passionate discussion of, well, just about anything and nothing.

But most especially, anything to do with bike racing, and gossip about the leading racers. And not only about Italian racers, but foreigners, for grandfather's bike frames were in high demand by elite riders in many countries. Any time there was a national caliber race in Italy, or a major tour abroad, it was hard to get the workers to focus on their work. They were too busy arguing about who would win or, after the race, arguing about who should have won, and in both cases, that the newspaper and television commentators who covered the race were complete idiots.

When the Giro came—every year around May—well, it might as well have been declared a three-week national holiday. In an effort to get at least some productivity out of the workers during the Giro, or maybe just because he loved to read it too, while working in his shop, grandfather had arranged for early morning delivery to his shop of fifteen copies of La Gazzetta dello Sport. Plus there were the TV monitors he installed so the workers could see the live coverage on RAI from their stations; even if this made foreign customers wait in the shop. Italians just took a spot to enter the conversation, and even forgot to buy something if their preferred biker lost. 'Nonno' Vincenzo Cristiani supported the Giro even if he could lose some immediate sales, because he always won new customers, enjoying the atmosphere of his shop so much that they came back to buy something another time.

Fabio's middle name was chosen by his parents to remind everyone of the family roots.

They were from San Giovanni, a beautiful town on the river in the Valle Brembana, the valley that runs north from Bergamo straight up to the mountains. San Giovanni was just north of San Pellegrino, home of the sparkling mineral water by the same name; San Pellegrino was just north of Bergamo; and Bergamo was just east of Milano. Grandfather's bike shop was always close.

Fabio had held a series of summer jobs in the San Pellegrino factory and with time, had worked his way into the office side of the operation. His innate aptitude for arithmetic (and later, mathematics) and his logical, calm mind, caught the attention of the owners. He became one of the key helpers in their finance department. From that, Fabio got a free education in international business and finance, because the 'Pellegrino' brand was well established in fashionable places around the world.

6

Not surprisingly, given the family's proximity to cycling, he knew how to ride a race bike. Fast. Very fast. Up and down hills, and on the flats. As a teenager, he had put his mind to riding and he trained around the Valle Brembana whenever he could.

It offered every possibility of terrain. One day there was to be a local race, sponsored by 'Pellegrino', a race of only 90 kilometers.

The parcours would run from the Pellegrino factory, straight up the Valle Brembana past San Giovanni, then left to climb up to the tiny village of Mezzoldo, at which began the crux: a 12 kilometer bitch of a climb, to the Passo San Marco, elevation 1989 meters with an average grade of about 8% and some much steeper ramps.

At the top of the pass the racers would turn around and descend the same route, with the race finish in the piazza of San Pellegrino's city hall. Trophies and cash prizes would be awarded to the three fastest climbers and to the overall winners of the race.

His grandfather would be there to support Fabio with his pirate flag, which he took to every race.

Fabio entered the race with bib number 81, as the lead rider for a local amateur team sponsored by his grandfather's shop. When his second cousin, Marco, heard about this, he also entered the race. Just a few years older than Fabio, he was a neo-pro rider with great prospects, just signed by a hot Italian pro team. Thrilled that Fabio was now racing, he hoped to speak with him after the race and persuade him to become a pro rider, like himself.

The day of the Giro de Pellegrino had arrived.

The entire valley was filled with cars, buses, campers, motorcycles, and of course - bikes. Team cars, team buses and all manner of transportation used by the *tifosi,* the rabid fans of Italian cycling.

Local bikers had ridden the course on their race bikes before it was closed, securing the best viewing spots on the climb and 'becoming' a part of the race, directly.

Fabio and the other riders lined up at the start at the Pellegrino factory. Marco was there, strong and sleek in his new team jersey and shorts. He told Fabio they had to talk after the race; Marco would introduce him to his whole team and to the owner.

The race began with a processional start of 3km so the *tifosi* would get a good view of the whole peloton. The real racing began 2km short of San Giovanni. They flew through the town and rode the 9km up the gentle incline of the Valle Brembana to Lenna at warp speed. By the time they started the real climbing at Mezzoldo, Fabio was in the breakaway group along with Marco, some of Marco's teammates, and the best climbers of the other Italian teams.

Marco was surprised how strong Fabio was; he muttered to a teammate, 'my cousin, the little shit, has probably done nothing but train on this climb the whole winter...I'll show him a thing or two'.

Marco decided he would let his cousin win the ascent, if he could; he wanted Fabio to have this so Marco could make a pitch to his team owner, to bring Fabio onto the team.

Marco thought he could win the overall race on the 45km descent back to San Pellegrino; the Italian *cognoscenti* viewed him as the best descender the peloton had seen in years. This would give a great story; the family that won this Giro, coming from no less than San Giovanni itself!

They passed the Rif. Madonna delle Nevi and started up the brutal incline of the hairpin turns, quickly rising above the tree line to approach the Passo di San Marco, still dusted with snow. Riding through a sea of *tifosi* and dodging their bodies and flags, Fabio arrived first to the 'finish line' at the pass. The announcer noted that he had made a record time in the ascent from Mezzoldo, being 12km of brutal climbing!

Fabio let his legs spin easily on the flat turnaround after the pass finish, waiting to see if Marco would arrive. He did, in the company of a group of four. Marco congratulated his cousin and said 'now it's my turn'. He sprinted off, launching himself down the mountain hairpins.

Fabio got scared on the descent, and lost time. Marco and his group of four were nowhere to be seen. There was still some snow on the edges of the road, in places where the sun did not shine.

His hands were freezing and almost numb. Some parts of the road were wet, water still trickling down the mountain brooks from the melting snow. He hadn't noticed any of these things on the ascent.

Crossing the finish line in San Pellegrino, he saw the race clock and that he made a very good time; probably he was in the top ten, excellent for an amateur. The sun was shining in the valley. The race officials gave him hot tea to warm him up. But there was a chill in the air. After a few sips of hot tea, Fabio allowed himself to take in the scene at the finish.

All he heard was the announcer's voice on the loudspeakers: '*Marco è morto! Marco è morto!*'

Fabio continued his work in Pellegrino's finance department. His bike reminded him of his cousin, and the pirate flag in his grandfather's shop reminded him that a dream could break at the beginning, in the middle or at the end of it...so it is better to not dream at all, and work. At least the water business was a good one, a clean and safe one.

Sometimes he thought that he should go back to riding again, and win for Marco, especially as he watched the livestrong bracelet that he never took off. But as fast as this thought came into his mind, even faster he took the thought out.

Fabio quickly became fluent in English. His linguistic proficiency expanded the possibilities for his self-education. An avid reader in the theory and practice of finance, he could buy the most important works in English, instead of waiting for a translation.

He decided that most of what was written in the field was utter rubbish. It was not literature, not good science or philosophy, and not even good business. There were a few exceptions. He once bought a book based on the reviewer's line, 'the book that rolled down Wall Street like a hand grenade'. Now, there was a 'must read'.

He read the book in one day, hoping the grenade would explode and reduce the gene pool of traditional investment bankers, whom he thought were morally bankrupt and even worse, intellectually bankrupt.

The author's thesis and anecdotes were brilliant and for him, entirely correct. Fabio followed the author closely; he seemed like a real thinker, a real philosopher. Inspired by the writings, he developed practical models for his current work, and used them to plan his future path. The water business seemed to be the right place for him.

As he was sure about it, he went out for a business lunch in Milano, with some Pellegrino customers. He ordered some water; they had only 'Fiji' in the fancy restaurant in Milano. He found San Pellegrino's water in New York, Lisbon, São Paulo, and Tokyo...

Thinking about the water from San Pellegrino in New York, Fiji in Italy, Norwegian water in Portugal, Portuguese water in Australia and all the oil, plastic, glass and transport costs from the water business. He remembered his first bike and how easy and simple life was. He felt sick.

He looked at his livestrong bracelet that he never took off and said, 'And they judge you?'

Nobody can understand a biker, without ever having ridden a bike.

He was very thirsty and drank the water he had available to drink. He would prefer to walk to the washroom and drink tap water, but it was a meeting with foreign customers, and he couldn't walk away. Feeling the smooth taste of the water, he took a decision.

Sometimes the world around you makes you do things you would never do out of the circumstances.

Fabio entered the Game.

Haidji

Chapter 5

The Council meeting was scheduled for dawn at the beginning of the third game day.

Alphabot opened the door.

White, Yellow, Red, Green, Blue, Purple and Black entered the room. The seven, wearing their togas in different colors, standing around the round white table. One after another, they sat down at their assigned chairs around the round table.

Alphabot brought them some coffee.

Black denied the coffee.

'Would you like some water, Sir?' Asked Alphabot.

'No, no coffee, no water...thank you', said Black.

Alphabot left the room and the meeting started.

They were more or less pleased with the results of the first two days, but needed to change some things about the betting system and also, about the street food.

Yellow had a suggestion, which he explained in too many words to the Council.

Besides betting on your favorite candidate number, which could be only one bet per ticket, and who knew how many would survive and die in each group or day, persons could only for this third game day bet on the composition of groups (of 20) of each day's group survivors.

The persons whose bet hit these 20 survivors in a group could win a prize that was more or less half the amount of the main prize, so he suggested. But because on the first step of the game it was possible and common that much more than 20 candidates would survive inside a group, he told them that he had considered carefully the mathematics of it all, and how the prize money would be allocated, so they would still rake a handsome profit.

He said they didn't need to bring in any experts in probability theory; they should just make this betting scenario for one day, to see the results. Green pretended he liked the idea.

Black said 'We'll vote about it...later.'

The Council also saw that street food vendors were starting to settle in, taking any available spot outside the Stadium gates. They were doing brisk business.

From monitoring the bracelets, the Council realized that the basic food and drink they offered in the Stadium was largely being ignored, in favor of the street food available outside.

People left the Stadium to buy it outside, coming back after. Not only were they losing potential profits, but also seats were left empty when persons went outside for food breaks, so it made the Stadium look less than full on the TV, while they took their food breaks.

Green had already a solution.

He had met with the most successful street food seller outside the Stadium and decided to invite him to meet the Council. He presented his idea to the Council; they agreed, in principle. He stepped outside the Council chamber, and returned with another man.

'This is Mr. Metz Wurss, known in the trade as 'Metz'. He is one of the top master chefs for street food in the whole world. He has designed a menu for the Stadium and he's here to tell us about it.'

Metz took a position at the Boardroom table, next to Green. 'Thank you, Members of the Council. Allow me to present the proposed Stadium cuisine. First we have the Suicide Dog. Next we have the Platform Stacker. To drink, we have the Bloodshake. All made with the freshest ingredients.

Each of them is available in meat, vegetarian or vegan options. Everything can be made fresh daily in the Stadium kitchen, under my personal supervision.

We use only the choicest cuts of fresh meat, and all other ingredients are 100% natural, fresh and of the highest quality.

And the Bloodshake is available in different flavors, with or without caffeine, or alcohol.

The Council asked if the Stadium kitchen was adequately equipped to prepare the cuisine. Metz answered quickly, 'Yes, no problem, and it's actually far more than adequate. The best cook is the one who needs only a very simple kitchen. I don't need Leonardo da Vinci's spaghetti fork, and I could cook anything using only some ancient Pompeii cooking utensils'.

Green was impressed.

Metz said, 'Oh, just one more thing. I have designed emoji icons for the menu items. I couldn't find any emoji for hot dogs, stacked sandwiches or fruit and protein shakes, so I thought we could use the game symbol, and change it around a little bit, into a dog sandwich or drink. People can text us their orders using the emoji and they won't even need to leave their seats. And this can also create a rumor that the food comes from the game.'

Red laughed ironically. 'Great marketing strategy!'

Black said 'we'll vote about it...now'.

Metz needed to go outside and wait in front of the door while they voted about the food. He could hear some crystal noises and something rolling, as would they be playing a kind of game inside the room. Invited to be part of the meeting again, Metz entered the room.

Green looked at Metz, and summarized their decision. 'Our decision is that our vendors need to carry food to the crowd, so the system you suggest is very good. But they can't have too many different things; less is more, so we decided for the Suicide Dog in meat and vegan, and the red fruits' Bloodshake, with or without alcohol.' Those would be the terms to Metz.

Metz felt that this was like going out of a Starbucks, to buy a coffee at the local greasy spoon. But he accepted their deal, to start selling his Suicide Dog and his red fruits Bloodshake, starting already on the next day, inside the Stadium. It would be a long night in the Stadium kitchen.

G

There was another matter for the Council. The question about whether, and how, to make one or two more rows of chairs in the Stadium.

The problem arose because now there were more and more persons outside the Stadium searching for non-existent real (or even fake) tickets, sleeping in tents in front of the entrance.

It was suggested the platform could appear to go a little bit higher up on the second step of the game, as part of the solution; for that, the ground should be excavated one meter deeper. It was easier to excavate the ground deeper and construct a new row or two of chairs along the bottom, instead of making new rows on the top sections, mostly because the structures at the top of the Stadium had been designed and optimized to the last millimeter by the Architect, Steven Laurence.

The Council wanted to make more space for the public, in order to sell even more real tickets.

Green pointed out that if the platform was too high, even just one meter higher, then some of the candidates' organs would be destroyed when they hit the ground, so the game would lose income from organ 'donations' (sales).

He reminded the Council that in addition to the usual buyers of living organs, they had a new client; a firm of doctors who were into bioengineering and who would prefer undamaged organs for their experiments. They decided they would need to vote about this issue, along with the betting issue, before end of their meeting.

About the condominium, they decided, for today's meeting at least, that the condominium system would be the same: after the first step, candidates would move into a new room and would participate in fitness lessons, and more intense neuro-linguistic programming 'training', and 'meditation'.

'The milk of amnesia is working well', said Green, 'no reason to increase it. Remember, in the past someone wanted to bring a pig into a courtroom to prove that it doesn't work on humans? What a joke! They probably forgot the mice experiments of 2007 or, what?'

'Probably...' said Yellow one, 'they probably forgot to mention it', and laughed in an ironic way.

'They probably forgot...to mention', said Black.

6

Before turning back to the major items of business for the day, the Council also voted on some other minor issues.

Each one of the seven Council members had a fixed place on the round white table, and in the center of the table was a glass ball, used for the voting system. The table color in front of them, for their respective part of the table, turned into the same color as their togas.

At the beginning of the meeting all their colors and voices were checked, to make sure that they were sitting in the right place.

In front of each member there was their polished metal sphere, about 3cm in diameter, which could be opened in two equal parts. Inside each sphere was a button that changed the color inside into red or green, by pressing it; red was for disapproval and green for approval. But the light would come on only after closing and opening the sphere again...to keep the privacy of the voting system.

Common voting systems are voting by majority rule, proportional representation, or plurality voting, but this Council used none of those systems.

Instead, only one sphere would decide the answer, and this was, as six of the seven council members believed, the proper corporate governance system to keep the outcome 'in the laps of the gods'. They believed that everyone could have the chance to decide alone and thus, a decision could legitimately be taken by any one of them (randomly and anonymously selected), no matter how many of the other members agreed or disagreed with the decision, and regardless of its impact on life, destiny, faith, or luck. This system, so they believed, should decide the way to go...and the words 'in the laps of the Gods' were written inside the clear tubes that would transport each voting sphere placed on the table, by each Council member, to the large crystal ball chamber in the middle.

The metal spheres came inside the tubes leading from each member's seat, and through a conduit were dropped into the crystal ball chamber, from the topside of the chamber. They start to mix in a clockwise direction and then against the clockwise direction, for a certain period of time, depending on the number of members present for a voting decision; with 7 members, there should be 7 seconds waiting after the first mix, and then 7 seconds in each direction, again and again, until one of the spheres passed into the tube on the bottom of the crystal glass ball, falling beneath it into a conduit into a crystal bowl, where the sphere would be opened automatically, showing its red or green light; and thus answering the question that had been voted on.

After the answer was received and recorded, the sphere would be closed and come again inside the crystal ball chamber, this time coming from the bottom, where, after a new mix, all the spheres came out through the top of the glass chamber, and back into the conduit tubes, which sent them back to their resting places in front of each council member. Except now, by some probability (perhaps), the seven members each had different metal spheres than the ones they used when they last had voted.

Now it was time for the Council's formal voting procedures to be implemented, to resolve the last items of today's business, using the voting system. Green for yes, and red for no, leaving the main decision, as six from the seven believed it should be, in the laps of the gods.

And on this day, the answer was 'no' to Yellow's suggestion and 'yes' to all the rest. It was a Green light, to all the Game Improvements, including for the platform to be one meter higher in the second game step, even with the risk of damaging some of the donation organs, by excavating the Stadium ground where necessary. Because it would be only one meter higher, the public's increased number of tickets, and the new bets they made, would more than cover some organ losses they might have because of it.

The Seven signed the protocol of the day.

Black, Purple, Blue, Green, Red, Yellow and White left the room. Alphabot closed the door, just as the sun was rising over the Stadium, for the third day of the Suicide Game.

Chapter 6

Candidate 3507

Anthony Henrik Gustav was a successful lawyer who had just rented a few more rooms in the building where he had his own office. And he had hired a few more trainees, to fill the rooms, dreaming about to hire the whole building, one day.

Some years back, he decided to expand his business. Back then, like nowadays, he spent much of his precious time on airplanes, from one side of the world to another, implementing major strategic business decisions. Back then, he had decided that his law firm, bearing his name, would be the first law firm to have offices in at least two different countries *and* with the countries being at least over 6000 miles away from each other and having entirely different languages. Law firms with offices in two or more countries were old news, but to have a firm that met this test would be 'news', and he was an innovator.

His symbol AHG, embroidered on the French cuffs of every shirt he owned, of course, was already well known in the lawyer world, as well as his ability to work long hours without a break, sleep on the chairs in his office, never miss a deadline, and forget to go home at night.

Working also Sundays, as would Sunday be the most important workday of the week, he lost sometimes the impression of time, but he never missed a client deadline.

Like many others in the legal game, he started from nothing, coming from an honorable but simple family, and thanks to his own efforts and a few good friends, he was where he was now, on the way to the very top echelons of the legal profession.

The lack of attention for his own family, which he compensated for with generous presents and unconsummated, platonic-only love flings with other women, were things he did not think about, as were they merely just the dust on the office window that he needed to ask to be cleaned one day; nothing really disturbing so long the sun, the moon or the stars could still shine through it, reminding him sometimes if it was day or night outside.

He was also looking for a new secretary, fat, of course, same as the last one, so as to not to raise suspicions about the nights he would spend, really working, while his wife was out with her friends or her personal trainer; the latter being more than just a platonic relationship, because AHG was never more than just part of the important decorations of status in her life.

Haidji

And she...she was the step he needed for the entrance into his law firm, coming from the right family, having the right contacts for him, and the money to help to pay for the first office abroad. So rich he was now, but his richness had limits. So they silently fulfilled all the clauses of their unspoken agreement about their personal lives, not needing to speak about it.

AHG's platonic lovers were organized at various times and locations, and being platonic they were also invited to his office, and they never created any conflict with his meager family life, because there was no family life at all.

In spite of, or perhaps because of, his brilliant legal mind, rapier quick wit and superhuman work ethic, he had become to some extent a creature of habit in what concerned the main patterns of his life actions. To sleep over his office chairs, was one of these habits.

He was working on one of his biggest cases, the biggest of all them. And he needed to think very carefully about his next steps; he thought again whether he could win again, like he always did, he never lost a case, but he also never had a big case like this. And this, this made him feel...afraid. Scared.

Recently, for perhaps the first time in his life, he had felt fear, which cut to the bone. This fear brought a certain sense of urgency. Being a man of action, not only a philosopher, he wanted to take immediate steps.

He knew that this case could allow him the expansion opportunity he dreamed about. It would float him and even better, his law firm and its logo AHG LLP, to the very top of the ocean of inflated egos in his profession. Some lawyers were predators; like sharks, they could never stop swimming, chasing their prey. Sometimes there were more sharks than readily available prey, and there were only so many hours in a day.

His case would be a game-changer. If he won it, he could create a global legal behemoth that would continuously scoop up clients and their dollars, even while he slept, as would they be endless schools of krill, silently scooped up in bulk by the giant baleen plates of a baleen whale.

But there was a problem. Actually, two problems. The problems were both double-edged swords.

One side gave him the bone-chilling fear, which he had come to like, because it gave him clarity. The other side presented clear and present dangers. And neither side was an illusion.

AHG was ruminating on his Two Problems.

Problem One: The case. He was now facing serious litigation, in the worst of all places, the United States. The litigation had not yet officially commenced, but he knew of it from private meetings with the plaintiffs' attorneys.

After some initial private talks, ostensibly aimed at achieving a quick settlement, he had asked them to hold off filing any court papers, and to keep the matter secret, for a few more days. And, perhaps surprisingly, they had agreed.

He needed to win the case, in order to create his legal behemoth.

Problem Two: He had received a tip from a trusted friend; there was, apparently, a plot to kill him. Talk about 'killing lawyers' was nothing new; lawyer jokes were almost more popular than blond jokes, and people bent on vilifying the legal profession misquoted Shakespeare's words endlessly: 'first thing we do, let's kill all the lawyers...' But a plot to kill him? Really? His source was impeccable.

He felt both edges of the sword, sharply. And continued ruminating on his Two Problems.

He could handle Problem One using his professional skills and network. He had already formulated his defense strategy; part of it included a storyline, to be published by a leading and influential US newspaper at the right time, to help shape public opinion and the jury pool's sympathies in his favor.

He prepared the storyline with the help of Marcel Michaelsen, his most trusted journalist friend.

The story ran like this, with some key names and places deliberately changed or omitted, in case the document would somehow fall into the wrong hands:

> For the last two decades Mr. Gustav has been battling Big Oil over an environmental disaster that happened in the jungles of Brazil. Two years ago, he won a $23 billion case against the oil giant, the kind of victory that even Texas and New York lawyers mostly dream of. But Big Oil has yet to pay the award. It has filed appeals at every step and has raised Constitutional arguments, arguing for Bill of Rights protections for multinational corporations headquartered in the USA. And now, Big Oil has launched a lawsuit against Mr. Gustav, alleging a criminal conspiracy to extort and defraud Big Oil. The trial will start in a few days, in a courtroom in Manhattan.

> In an exclusive interview with this reporter, Mr. Gustav for the first time spoke publicly about the case and what he says is Big Oil's attempt to assassinate his character. He even says he's heard Big Oil has hired enforcers to make sure he doesn't win the case. While this might sound like the ravings of a persecuted, self-appointed Saint, Mr. Gustav does have a serious following among environmentalists and environmental lawyers. He and his supporters say he is being persecuted for exposing Big Oil's dubious environmental record.

Haidji

Big Oil has accused Mr. Gustav of engineering the
ghostwriting of crucial reports submitted to the
Brazilian court that decided the case, and of bribing
key Brazilian witnesses. Big Oil also alleges that
Mr. Gustav held secret meetings with Brazilian
judges who were involved in the case. On the other
hand, Mr. Gustav insists that Big Oil's predecessor,
a foreign subsidiary of another Big Oil company, cut
through the Amazon and spilled oil and other toxic
chemicals from the drilling operations into pristine
rain forests, rivers and creeks, leaving behind a
toxic mess that not only caused serious health
problems for the local population but also caused
one of their largest businesses, the water company
Aguamazonas to fail, losing billions of dollars of
future revenue from sales to their international
markets.

Mr. Gustav says he traveled to Brazil in 1998 and
saw what he described as an apocalyptic site,
almost like a war zone, with jungle lakes and creeks
filled with oil, children walking barefoot on oil-
covered roads, and the Aguamazonas factory shut
down entirely.

But Big Oil never accepted the validity of the court's
judgment, and it funded a documentary film, which
essentially stars its CEO and some Brazilian
employees, in an effort to portray Mr. Gustav as a
charlatan.

Mr. Gustav has now countersued Big Oil for fraud and extortion, accusing Big Oil of defamation, corruption, bribes and threats to officials not only in Brazil, but also in America. He denies that he has ever crossed any ethical line. He is confident he will prevail, after the trial starts in Manhattan. 'I have a surprise for them', he says. 'I don't think this case will go on for months, which is what Big Oil wants. I think it will be over much more quickly than that'.

AHG and his journalist friend Marcel Michaelsen felt good about the story. They had already hired jury consultants, all of who told them they figured that no American jury was ever going to find against a lawyer who had gone up against big oil for years and years, and won.

Nevertheless, AHG was scared about the case and the upcoming trial and, for the first time in his life, he was afraid to death. Marcel's help was invaluable; probably it was the only thing keeping him strong.

Together with Marcel, he found a solution for Problem Two. An unusual solution. But he knew that Marcel was a friend of some Council Member in the Suicide Game.

He needed a place to hide; and together they figured out that at least for a while, what better place could you escape to hide from someone who wants to kill you, than a place where persons kill themselves?

Using Marcel's connection to the Council member, and subtracting some values from his Swiss account and adding them to another Swiss account, AHG entered the Suicide Game.

He was a lawyer and he knew that it would be best to trust his journalist friend, but not to tell his own lawyer about his decision.

Consciously and deliberately, he decided to become a Suicide Game candidate, in order not to be killed and maybe, who knows? Win the game. Not something you'd want to tell your lawyer, even if you trusted him.

Haidji

Chapter 7

Step 1 – Day 3

Alessandra did not leave the Stadium on the first day.

It wasn't possible for her to go out of the Stadium.

She found a vacant room, behind the scenes, with a small garden with flowers, and stayed there with the baby. The baby had an electronic bracelet, but it did not work when she tried to exit with the baby in the break after the first jump, and she did not have her own bracelet, because she took it off, angry after denying the job; an impulsive reaction, throwing it away from her.

They would not let her out, because the game already started, and she would probably be arrested if she would try to go out of there again, having tried once and failed.

Elisabeth, the woman working at the Stadium entrance, had told her about the room, mentioning that she could not let her go out with the baby, thinking that it was Alessandra's child.

Something was wrong with the baby's bracelet and Alessandra did not have her own anymore, and rules, rules are rules no matter which game it is, we need to follow the rules.

Elisabeth was also the chief of the Stadium guards, in a non-official way; she could make some rules and break others up to a point, but she couldn't let someone without bracelet in or out.

But...she could help Alessandra to stay at the Stadium, inside a safe place for the baby, and would show her the way to this vacant room, pretending that Alessandra would also be working for the game soon.

Elisabeth had kids herself, and the baby needed to sleep, so she showed Alessandra the way to the vacant room, that was clean and minimalistic. No dangers for the baby. Elisabeth also asked the workers to find a baby bed for the baby. Or to make one. They made one with pieces from some extra Stadium seats. Six seats together and some work on it, made a baby's bed.

There were some flowers on the window sill, and the room had a small bathroom and, by a small hallway, she could reach a cooking space, a kind of kitchenette, used by the security guards while watching the football games and other events on the external TV feeds, to pass the time on their breaks. The solution for her was to stay there until the end of the game. For her, the baby was safer with her than with the Red Cross volunteer she saw walking around. He had a strange look. She noticed that, even when he was running in another direction. He did not seem like someone that would take care of a baby; something was strange with him.

Cassandra noticed Alessandra walking with the baby as she entered to work; she turned her head and smiled to the baby, but did not really see them as she passed them, almost brushing their side. She was thinking about a way to enter into the condominium where candidate number 2252 was, and she also wanted to know what was really going on in there.

She had spent the evening thinking about the Game, and thinking about her candidate. She had stopped at the condominium entrance on the day before, on her way home. But her entrance was denied, her electronic bracelet allowed her to enter only the Stadium, so there must be a bracelet or special program only for the Condominium Staff, she reasoned.

Disappointed with her failure on the day before, she was going out in a work break, to buy some Starbucks coffee. The entrance woman, Elisabeth, stopped her to ask if she might have some clothes at home for a friend of hers and told her, because she liked to chat, that they were looking for kitchen personnel, night workers, to prepare the candidates' meals for the next days, only two or three hours part-time, and gave her the phone number to contact them for the job.

Elisabeth liked to chat...a lot. Working together with the entrance guards, she felt like the Stadium's guardian, as would she be the guardian in the entrance to heaven or hell.

Elisabeth also described the room where Cassandra could bring the clothes for her new friend, Alessandra, the next morning. For Elisabeth, real life was full of friends, a person just needed to speak to her longer than a minute to be accepted in her life friends' list. Life was beautiful and she had already made more than 1000 friends in her first workday at the entrance, but some were close friends. Like Alessandra and the baby, and Cassandra, of course.

Cassandra called the number and applied for the work. It was a fast interview; she was a good professional and already part of the Game staff, in the sense that her personal data was already in the game database.

She told them that she could start right away, already on the same night if necessary; they told her that her existing electronic bracelet would be reprogrammed so she could also enter this part of the game without further security checks.

In the morning of the third day, Cassandra stopped at Alessandra's room to bring her some of her own things, and they spoke a little.

Alessandra did not tell Cassandra how she found the baby, only that she couldn't leave the Stadium and she needed to stay there until game's end, because she did not have her own bracelet anymore and the baby's one was broken...'Kids...!'

Cassandra respected people's private space and did not ask more about it. Almost late going to work, she was also not really interested; her mind was somewhere else.

Cassandra was smiling while preparing the candidates, but it was a kind of nervous smile, because after the fourth day there would be a day's break, after which the second step of the Game would start; so with a little bit of good luck, perhaps she could see her candidate again, maybe already this evening...and luck seemed to be on her side, for now.

The public was still very interested in the Game, and even at home people were still jumping up from the couch upon hearing the Hostess' voice, when she, the Hostess, promised surprises for the second step of the Game, higher prizes in cash, higher payoffs in the bets, and even more new surprises.

T-shirt sellers were making huge profits in front of the Stadium and now, even the crowd seemed to wear uniforms, wearing black t-shirts with the orange symbol on the front and the words Suicide Game on the back, printed with a fluorescent orange color.

The Hare Krishna group had left their spot near the main entrance, having abandoned their previously undisclosed idea to sell incense and deciding instead to walk among the crowd to sell lighters, which were more useful inside the Stadium, especially in the afternoons and evenings. They decided to attract attention by going back to their spot and continuing to sing their mantras when the game countdown clock started at 50.

A teenagers' group on Facebook was organizing a contest, to create a song for the event, and to make YouTube videos about it.

Haidji

The tenth and last group of this third day was ready to jump.

And the voice of the beautiful Hostess rose again over the mob's murmur:

'At the end of this successful day, I introduce to you, the last group of the day. They were excited all day, being prepared to be part of your day and jump for you. And now, they are finally here. Now they can show you what they can, using all their concentration, focusing on their goal, they are now an active part of...

SUICIDE GAME!

The new game
The new mania
8000 candidates and
Only one will survive
Only one can win!
Live from the Night Stadium
Nothing compares to what you'll see here
Nothing compares to what you'll watch
You already chose your candidate,

You have Made your bet

To be part of a

New and unexpected game

Now it's time to let it all be in the laps of the gods

And when the bell rings…it is time to jump for your life!

10…9…8…7…6…5…4…3…2…1!

JUMP!'

One second before the group was to jump, while still on the platform, candidate number 4957 fainted. This was something wholly objectionable and inadmissible, and that should be urgently investigated; but first, immediately covered up.

The Hostess came immediately to pull her softly, over the edge of the platform, to create the impression of a jump, so as to avoid risk that the game could be stopped for a breach of the rules (or at least of the mathematical odds); the Council saw it through the internal video system, and immediately directed the camera and projection operators to exclude all images of candidate 4957 from all the projections. It was good that the Hostess and the images' staff were well trained for unexpected situations.

The fainter was a woman, and before the survivors' group arrived on the ground, another staff member was already there, hugging her as one of her feet was twitching, almost touching the ground, and carrying her away from there swiftly, so fast that the public would not notice that she had fainted and not really jumped.

The cameras were aimed in another direction while a champagne glass was removed from one of the celebration tables by one of the models wearing a blue dress; knocking it in her haste, it spilled over the table and fell onto the sand on the ground and shattered, but before they brought the table to the platform.

So, most probably, no one noticed that there were only 910, and not 911, celebrating the victory of the survivors, and her number would get lost, perhaps, among the losers, and maybe nobody would figure out that she was alive, or had not died.

She was not there anymore to celebrate her victory, or maybe they would think that she was out of the game for other reasons; this was an unanticipated problem, with potential implications for the betting system and the odds makers.

Should her number be among the winners or losers? One of the game administrators began to get a headache. On the surface, it appeared they had covered up this problem with their quick action. But underneath, maybe it would come to light, somehow.

They brought her back to the condominium with a minivan, with blacked out windows, where a doctor was already waiting for her.

Haidji

Chapter 8

Candidate 4914 – Jens Plaato

He was agnostic. About everything, it seemed.

He believed that the question of whether there is a greater power, whether called God or anything else, never was and never will be resolved.

Sometimes, since it is a question about 'God'...he would say empirically, 'I do not know, and you, how do you know?'

In other matters...such as dealing with the problems of their government...he would say, 'I do not know, but you also do not know.'

Sometimes, in personal matters, he would say, listlessly... 'I do not know, but why does or should it concern me?'

In serious governmental problems—which it was, to some extent, his responsibility to fix—he was also agnostic... 'I do not know how to solve this, but for that matter, who does?'

And: 'Sometimes the way is to hire consultants, to do modeling. The idea on how to solve these problems, I do not know.

But we can create a solution to solve this problem, and to achieve a greater understanding of what is the problem, and we must do this before we try to find a solution for it.

Maybe we should ask them what to say even before we have a problem, to have the answer ready, for whatever it is.'

'I see, I fix, I solve it.'

It was his campaign speech. That meant: all I need is my charm and presence.

Sometimes rhetoric was just another way to lie and impress persons, and he knew this.

He used to lie without thinking about other persons' feelings, caught by the moment and whomever he wanted to impress in front of him. Many times he just used to say something that the person in front of him would like to hear, with no idea about the consequences of his words. Words are not actions, he used to think, words are just words, we don't need to do what we say we will, or to feel what we say later on. I speak only for immediate results. The rest around me I can see, fix and solve later; I dominate rhetoric. What's important is to catch the momentum and the opportunity to make whomever it is love me. I see the opportunity. I fix the moment. I solve the rest later on.

Of course he never spoke about his own views openly. Of course sometimes he hurt persons he didn't want to hurt, and needed to 'see, fix and solve' later on. But it was as it was. Finally, he was a politician; he knew well how to use all the words, and to be agnostic, all at the same time.

Haidji

Agnostic, also about his own feelings about the world. He believed it important to be always agnostic, so he would be widely understood, even for those who do not know the meaning of his words, he could convince them about his own non-existent truth. I see...I fix...I solve it. Now or later, I do it.

He also defended the nude as a rich and perfect unity of body and spirit, and as an important part of the progress of a nation.

He could also go for some environmental restrictions in the name of progress...after all; he was agnostic; as, in all its aspects, was his life.

In sum, Plaato was a master chameleon, a mimic, a complete unoriginal. He had a photographic memory, which he could have put to good use. Instead he used it to remember key words and phrases he read in philosophical and political treatises, which he then adjusted and passed off as his own, or spewed out *verbatim* in a convulsion of literary name-dropping; in both cases, timing his delivery for maximum credibility with his audience.

In his case, at least, beauty probably really was not even skin-deep; anyone with a meaningful soul who got to know him well enough would inevitably see the nothingness beneath the surface.

Yet in spite of that, he remained popular among a certain crowd, a frequent dinner guest at their parties. The fact that he was good-looking also helped his popularity among the *unintelligensia*.

Indeed, he was enjoying his new fame as the top-ranked man on a new Rumor site, 'YourPoliticianBoyfriend', which ranked the 21 hottest Politicians in the Country.

The site featured his photo and a quote from him upon hearing of his selection: 'most unusually for a politician, I'm entirely speechless. It's a tremendous honor to be selected, thank you, and very reassuring to know that if the current attempts at political reform end up breaking our economic system altogether, at least some of us have a sporting chance to accomplish something in other ways. I see...I fix...I solve it!'

The site also gave its own commentary on each politician ranked. Of Plaato, Politician #1, the experts said: 'it is as if, from birth, he deliberately planned every step of his life in order to sit atop the PoliticianHottie list. The media digs him, and also Hollywood movie stars, and we imagine all the other politicians hate him'.

But Plaato did have some detractors in the herd. Unlike most of the *unintelligensia*, their bullshit detectors were finely tuned. 'He is a half-man', said one.

Haidji

He explained: 'a half-man is not someone who does not have an opinion, just someone who does not take any risks for it'. 'So, then', said another, 'Plaato is really a zero-man, no?'

But for him, this was just jealousy end envy. He was just the best. Some persons cannot deal with other persons' success.

He entered the Game because it was good for his image.

He wanted to be on top of the platform, jumping into his public's embrace.

He did not judge things, only God can judge, and he was agnostic. If he would survive or die, he did not know, but who does?

We all die one day.

So he entered the Game. He was at the top of the Hottie list, but that wasn't enough. He wanted to be the first politician in the Game, so he could be in first place everywhere.

Haidji

Chapter 9

It was an emergency; the council needed to meet.

Alphabot was working somewhere else; they opened the door alone. And there was no coffee.

White, Yellow, Red, Green, Blue, Purple, Black.

All seven wearing their togas in seven different colors entered the room and took their assigned places around the round table.

Black asked the other members: No coffee? No water?

No, no coffee, no water for us today, Black, Alphabot is not here, said Green.

Alphabot is not here? Where is he?

He is working on something else, said Green, but you don't drink coffee, why do you care?

Lets start the meeting, said Red; we have more important things to deal with now than the fact that there is no coffee here today.

There was a kind of fear in the air, as would something new disturb the presence of death in the game.

How could someone faint in the middle of a jump?

They brought the woman from the condominium to the nearest hospital to find out what happened, because the doctor at the condominium couldn't find out. They brought her with a normal car and civilian-clothed staff, to avoid the press attention that was always around the condominium, as would the candidates already be major celebrities.

With a common simple blood test, they found out.

She was pregnant. Pregnant? How could a woman be pregnant? Yes, a woman could be pregnant, they forgot about that.

Months ago, as they were choosing the game candidates, looking over their applications, Purple had suggested a quarantine period before the game started, because of this type of event, 'and the possibility of other diseases', had added the Blue Council member; but now, it was all too late, and they had deadlines, so that would probably not happen.

And Diseases?' asked the Yellow Council member. 'Diseases? They all want to die, why to worry about diseases?'

And the Red Council member said, 'did you forget about the organ donations (sales)? Of course they should all be tested for diseases, and all be healthy candidates. But quarantine isn't important, with all modern tests and equipment we have'.

'Anyway', continued Red, 'you cannot competently decide to die if you're not really alive and healthy, but our tests showed they were all healthy, all 8000 of them, including the ones that already died—but pregnancy isn't a disease—so, I guess our doctors forgot to think about this small detail of the female being's life.'

And Blue calmed them down. 'Disease or not disease, doesn't matter how they want to call it, pregnant persons could not participate in the game. We cannot be responsible for killing innocents.'

He continued on with his advice that they needed to have some moral rules in this suicide game, for God's sake.

And now...they needed to vote. What to do? Should they allow or not allow pregnant women to take part in the Game?

Should they pretend that they did not know it, the fact of pregnancy?

'We'll vote about it...now', said Black.

Or should they test all female candidates and send all the pregnant women back home?

'But this would be really inconvenient', said Red, who agreed that they should administer the pregnancy test, 'But it would be very inconvenient to remove all their numbers from the already printed bet lists. We would need to print them all again, and worse, this would wreak havoc on the existing odds'. He continued to explain; it was easy to remove numbers after a game day, because all the candidates were already separated by their scheduled jump day and sequencing.

But to do it like that? To find some numbers among thousands...? Someone will need to make the extra hours for that, and they needed to pay for that, and for the silence of the pregnant women, about all that was happening in the condominium and game's backstage places

'We'll vote about it...now', said Black.

And they voted.

The metal spheres came from each Council member to the crystal ball, traveling inside the conduit tubes and then dropping into the crystal ball chamber, from the topside of the chamber. They started to mix in a clockwise direction, and then against the clockwise direction. Since all 7 Council members were present and voting, after the first mix there were 7 seconds of waiting, and then the ball chamber spun again, 7 seconds in each direction, again and again...until.

Until one of the spheres fell into the conduit on the bottom of the crystal ball, traveling via the same tube into a crystal bowl, in the center of the boardroom table. The sphere then opened automatically, to show the red or green light, thus answering the question that had been put to the vote.

And the answer was green: 'Yes', the pregnant women should be sent home.

After the answer, the sphere came again inside the crystal ball, from the bottom, and after a new mix of all the spheres, they came out through the top of the chamber, back into their conduit tubes, which sent them back to their original places, in front of each Council member.

Four of them had voted 'no', and only three had voted 'yes'.

The final answer was 'yes'.

The Yellow Council member seemed to be relieved as the answer came out, because he was unsure and had changed his answer three times (he voted yes at the end), while Green seemed to be angry. Because most of the times that he voted against something, his vote never seemed to be the chosen one; maybe the Gods were never on his side?

Upset, he started a discussion: 'and what about parents? Shall their kids see them jumping in the Stadium?'

Purple answered that kids are not allowed in the Stadium, of course; they knew there were some teenagers with fake IDs, but nothing out of normal life.

'Not allowed in the Stadium...kids', said Black, as would he be memorizing the sentence.

'Yes', said Yellow, 'but kids can see everything in the media and by using their internet devices, and nobody seems to be worried about it.

'We cannot be responsible for that; it is their parent's choice to take part in the game. What about war? Parents also don't always come back. Kids see about that in the media too. And sometimes, in some countries, there is not even free will to be a soldier, but there is a legal obligation. And here, it is free will. Candidates applied for entry into the game. It is their own decision.'

They didn't need to vote on this point. Parents could be candidates, of course. They cannot be responsible for what kids see at home, just like governments cannot be responsible if the kids see what happens in the media, when they send their parents into war somewhere. But kids were not allowed inside the Stadium. Of course not. This would be terrible and unacceptable. Some almost 18-year old teenagers with fake IDs were allowed to enter in bars and discos. But kids in the Stadium, no.

Then Green had good news that made them change the subject in the meeting, and inside their minds too.

Metz' creations were selling almost as fast as the kitchen could make them. They had more than 90% of the Stadium ticket-holder's market. And hardly any of the Game staff were going outside for food anymore. But there was also the outside public, which couldn't enter the Stadium, increasing day after day; shouldn't they think about selling Metz' creations outside, also?

Metz had agreed to stop selling outside when he entered into the agreement to sell his special new creations inside the Stadium.

And they voted about it.

Outside sales, 'yes, starting with the second game step, provided that persons who pay so much for their seats inside, should have priority rights'.

They were happy with the decision: already having the same amount of public consumers around the Stadium, as inside it, it was good to sell outside too.

'Very well done', said the Purple Council member. 'And the marketing strategy works. Fresh corpses—the freshest meat available anywhere, heheheh! Fresh blood and fresh meat. Metz is not only a good cook, he is a marketing genius, and this is nowadays more than 50% of the food business. Or sometimes even 90%. Without great marketing, you can be the best chef, but all you get at the end is the remainders from your competitors' garbage pails.'

G

The Council continued the meeting after taking a break, having gone outside to the food trucks to drink a coffee.

No coffee, Black? Asked Green.

No, said Black. No coffee...no water.

Unexpected...that 12 candidates...were pregnant, including the one that fainted.

They needed to pack their things. Council staffers would ensure they signed another confidentiality agreement about all they saw inside the complexes and the game. It was best that they would sign after dinnertime and be sent home in the early morning, and they would have a special session of neuro-linguistic programming before dinner.

And the departing candidates would also receive a 'consolation prize' check with a 5-figure sum; because they would not die so soon; they would need some money to keep living, and to take care of their kids.

Numbers 4957, 7821, 3287, 5432, 1452, 1473, 0061, 2982, 7011, 6253, 4216, 1045.

All were out of the competition.

The Council noticed that most of them already jumped once and survived, hopefully they would not find some of them among the already dead ones.

On the fourth day there would be three candidates less in the game. 'Hopefully nobody will notice this sad fact', said a Council member.

And then, they needed to vote about the diamonds. With that, their work would be done, the major decisions for the second step of the game.

As for the diamonds: Red was against, it was too weird; but all the others, even the Green Council member, voted 'yes', because it was simply a great idea, that should be announced soon, in time for the first day of the second step of the Game.

They left the room and forgot to close the door. Alphabot passed by later on, to clean the room.

And closed the door, after he left the room.

Some workers, dressed all in black, needed to spend the night working to remove the twelve numbers from all virtual and paper voting tickets and lists, and amending other Game records. The pregnant women, with a new life inside of them, were declared as 'death' in the game records.

Haidji

Chapter 10

Candidate 4918 - Sarah Mondstein

It was a cold night. Sarah woke up and covered herself, but she had caught a cold anyway. Tall, blond, pale like the moonlight on winter nights, she went to work the next morning, also with a cold.

She walked around the office to her desk, with Aspirin, lemon, anti-inflammatory medicines, ginger, honey and maybe even antibiotics, who could tell what was in her collection?

Her stock of potions looked almost as impressive as that of a small pharmacy. She had all this inside her bag, and she put it all over the desk; she had stopped at the pharmacy and another small store on the way to work, to get what she thought she needed for her cold.

The man who worked in the pharmacy was one of her usual lovers, so she could buy anything from him, all without prescription.

Money, charm and a blond smile, were the tools she used to have all she wanted in life. She made a cup of tea, took her medicaments, and decided that she should feel better soon.

Sarah grew up with her parents, but her mother died as she was turning 14. Her father was absent. Her relationships were doomed to disaster even before they started. She used to fall in love in a way that turned defects into qualities in the first days (or nights), and then her lovers' good qualities would become fundamental and fatal character faults, after a while.

She was bored, bored about not finding the perfect lover, or (from comments she had heard) maybe not being one. Bored with making excuses to herself about their age, inches, and the very real fears and traumas of each lover she captured.

She didn't have time for her own fears and therefore, in her mind, this justified her not caring about other persons' feelings.

After the first or second time making love with her lovers, her boredom with them would start to set in, and then she felt sick, so she would sink into the bath tub and rub her skin to take their smell away, hoping to erase her memories, along with her own wishes and desires, down the drain, faraway from her daily life.

Sarah would see the pharmacy guy, again, but only for small talk; her coldness was overtaking her now, so he would soon see that her apparent beauty and warmth was an illusion, as clear and icy cold as her touch would soon feel to him.

Haidji

Maybe the next time she would send her Personal Assistant, Anna, to the pharmacy, who as the inheritor of her old computer, out of season clothes and last mobile phone model, was also happy to date some of her ex-lovers sometimes, trying to be like her.

Sarah called it recycling. It was good for the work environment.

Sarah became very successful creating avatars and destinations for Second Life. So much success she had, in her business life: her avatars were touching, strong, hard, funny and lovely at the same time and persons loved the destination places she made; but she did not know how to touch someone intimately, in a caring way, and she certainly did not like to sleep close together, whether or not they made love.

She typically vomited out her lovers on the second or third date, in the same way that she would sometimes vomit her food after lunch or dinner to keep her figure.

This was her drug, the eternal search and unsatisfied hunger, with control over herself, and only herself, being her only real dream.

Searching for something that could satisfy her hunger, the pursuit of something she already knew was unknown to her...this was her drug, and the dream she lived.

She lived on the catwalk of life without looking around and really seeing anything, walking over the cold ice of lonely nights without really feeling anything, searching for warmth inside her fancy clothes as if they would reflect her biological body heat and then deliver to her, as a complete whole, the designer shards and shadows of her own dreams.

And this was how she was.

Until the first time she entered the door of 'Update'.

She had heard about it. 'Update' was an insider tip, a 'must do it' for singles. And she thought that it would be exactly the right thing for her.

She was excited, it *was* exactly was she was looking for, she thought the first time she was filling out the Update forms.

It wasn't a date. It wasn't a normal blind date.

And it wasn't an arrangement made by her friends where she needed to spend the morning or sometimes until lunchtime with more or less idiots, and note a phone number she would never call again, hearing the two most stupid questions that all men ask, but that still are the most stupid questions that a man could make:

Did you like? Did you come?

Haidji

As would a man not know how good or bad he has been, or that a woman would answer always 'yes' to both, to be polite, saying the truth only if she would be inside a serious relationship were they could speak openly about all...or answering 'no' and making it all worse than it was, in case she wanted to hurt him.

Update was the right place for her.

The form was easy to fill out. Just tick any or all of the boxes next to your preferences.

Gender: Male.

Body Type: Athlete.

Ectomorph or Mesomorph: she ticked both boxes.

Primary Racial features: Caucasian.

Secondary Racial features: no preference.

Activity? Here she could check any of about 50 boxes. Heterosexual. Oral. Vaginal sex. Hard core. But not rough.

Perfume for him: L'Eau par Kenzo pour homme.

Her perfume: Dolce&Gabbana pour femme.

Safety: she ticked the 'no disease' box.

The form required her to authorize a quick blood test that would be discreetly administered by the Update administrators before her first 'update'.

After a few days, they called her. She had an 'update' scheduled.

G

She entered the dark room and walked to the bed.

He was already there, she couldn't see him in detail, there was enough light to see the form of things, but not enough to recognize someone. She could see him as would he be a shadow figure and she felt his presence and perfume in the room.

He came closer to her and his hand touched her shoulder, pulling her closer to him, fast and unexpected.

His lips sliding over her neck, he whispered something.

'Princess...'

Like a cold shower running over her skin...She had crossed 'hardcore', and he whispered...princess?

Haidji

This was overwhelming. She thought about leaving the room and complaining about it, going one step back; but he pulled her closer to him, holding her hair together inside his hand, pulling her head into a kiss...it was...intense.

It was a mixture between sex and romantic, as would she break all her barriers and fears, and suddenly she couldn't stop or think about it, she lost her barriers and discovered how...how to touch a man, how to feel.

It was, as would all she was looking for be there, in front of her. Inside a dark room, a hormonal update with a stranger.

On her second update, she decided to cross something more romantic, because she liked to hear him whispering into her ears and thought maybe that was a reason to like the situation, of course, and not him as a person. She wouldn't fall in love with a complete stranger.

She entered the room and her soul was thirsty to hear the same voice again...and it was...his voice...the same man. In a more romantic situation. And she loved it.

On the third update, she did not know what boxes to tick or cross. She was afraid to cross something he disliked and also afraid that maybe he did not like to have been with her a second time, so he would change his preferences on the forms, to not meet her again.

She was scared as she entered the room.

Her legs were feeling weak, her head turning in circles. She did not know if she could stay, but she was too afraid and too dizzy to run away.

But he came closer; it was the same perfume...he touched her face, and what sounded like the same voice, whispered into her heart and ears... 'Princess'.

Some persons fall in love first and have sex after the third date.

Some persons have sex first and break their hearts because it wasn't what they expected it to be.

Some persons never seem to be in love and others are always into it.

Sarah felt completely in love on her third update.

And this was so overwhelming for her that she did not know how to deal with the situation.

She did not know his name, phone number or address, or where he worked, or what he thought about life.

All she knew was how it was to feel his skin under her hands and how it felt to be close to him. And to stay there, without the wish to leave. To feel his skin close to her and hear his voice whispering things into her heart's ear.

She asked at the entrance of Update who he was, but all client details were private and confidential.

Not even her money could help her to find more information about him.

All she could do was to schedule a next update and then, maybe ask him his name? If he would be there again? If he would tell her who he was? If he would like to meet her outside of there?

She had a bad headache and sent Anna to the pharmacy to get something for her. Anna was happy to meet the Pharmacy guy, they were dating. She brought her something. But it did not help her. She couldn't take him out of her mind. Not even a hot bath helped her.

So, she scheduled a new update. The room was dark. The perfume was the same one she crossed in the Update forms, but the man was another one.

It was someone else.

Sarah went back home, sick and broken.

Then she tried again; but again, it wasn't him.

Maybe on the third try?

It wasn't him again.

Sure that she would never see him again; she figured out that she had nothing more to lose. Because she already lost everything she had found.

To fall in love, for the first time in her life, give herself to a stranger and never see him again, was too much for her already broken soul. She couldn't go back to the life she had before, but she also couldn't move on.

She was asymmetric before she met him, but she did not realize it; she was used to being asymmetric. It was something intense and new for her to feel complete.

She was complete inside a dark room with a stranger, and now she was feeling asymmetric again; conscious about the emptiness in her life, she felt hurt in a full way, as would part of her body have been taken away. As would something have cut her body in two, with her being conscious and alive.

All of that was incomprehensible for her. To realize that also she, not just others, could have real feelings; deep incomprehensible feelings, which she could not fulfill in the normal ways she used to fulfill her basic needs.

She couldn't live this way of life. And couldn't go back to the way she used to live before.

She was trying to be practical and realistic about her situation.

Without the courage to kill herself, Sarah decided to jump into the Suicide Game.

Chapter 11

Step 1 - Day 4

Cassandra was tired from her first night's work in the condominium kitchen, the night before, to help prepare the candidates' dinners.

She was thinking about the kitchen while she prepared her candidates with John, who had an especially good mood this day; waiting for the next day, it would be a rest day for him, he had the day off...but all this tension in time was making John a little bit depressed.

Rushing into perfection, he wanted his work to be appreciated, but to make them all look alike wasn't always easy... 'Imagine that on another day, a candidate wasn't raised into the jumping list. Can you imagine?' he muttered to himself. 'He wasn't raised! How much makeup he needed to make his face look smooth and pure like ivory? How much of my precious time and energy he took!' Oh my God...he really needed a day off. The lack of respect for his work was making him feel cranky; he was a makeup artist, not a locksmith!

The game needed to start soon and much work was there to do: 'We don't have time to be cranky, John!'

'I cannot even be cranky?

If I am happy and laugh too loud, or if I am sad and cry sometimes, I am bipolar! In this world, to laugh is to be a hysteric and to cry is to be a depressive! To laugh or cry isn't normal anymore. Better I make up myself today, like the candidates...and no words will come out of my mouth until the sun goes down!'

The game needed to start soon and work was there to do, 'We don't have time to be cranky, John!'

Cassandra said, 'your work is great, John! The best. They all will look like white piano ivory keys.'

'As if piano keys would be round', said John, 'Perfect! They must be perfect!'

'Now just make the Symbol between the eyebrows, John. Your day off is coming tomorrow. They are all perfect! You are a great artist!'

A shadow of a smile broke on John's face.

Great artist! This made his mood better! His work was being recognized! And he looked at the next candidate and worked in silence for a while. Then he continued working and singing a melody of a song that a friend's son had written, for a contest on Facebook.

With John rescued, at least for a while, before his next crisis, Cassandra wandered back to her own thoughts.

G

Cassandra remembered the night before, in the condominium kitchen...the food, there was something wrong with the food there.

Every tray had a number written on the bottom of the right side, and they always needed to make the same doses of food in each tray for each candidate.

The room was full and she saw candidate 2252. She was happy to see him alive, but he seemed so far away, like all the others, and he didn't notice her or the others around him; they all were eating in silence, as would the room be the wake room of a cemetery.

There was a kind of sauce that was always the last thing they would make over the candidates' plates. A transparent sauce that tasted like bitter vinegar: she tasted a drop of it, just a drop; she was always interested to improve her kitchen skills, she exclaimed to the kitchen workers around her, when she tasted the sauce. But there was also a note about one candidate, number 3507, that had an allergy to the sauce. So she decided to write under that note that candidate 2252 was also allergic, just in case he could be and also, because she thought nobody could really enjoy eating this meal with this vinegar sauce all over it.

Why a sauce that tastes like vinegar, over the food? Does this taste well? But there were no complaints about the sauce so, maybe, this was one of these fashionable things, like sushi once was, that she never understood herself, but that happens in the world.

Suddenly everybody loves the same food, even if years before they wouldn't like it. In some parts of the world persons eat horses and snails, but vinegar sauce over everything? It was strange. Not everything is just bread and salad, where vinegar was great; something was strange inside this kitchen.

From her last evening's thoughts she remembered only that she had a good night's sleep, so she was probably just overtired, because she didn't even remember her way back home, and she woke up in the morning on her bed, with her yesterday clothes on.

But this morning, she was late to work, she needed to go and calm John down, and she had no time to think about things. She had taken a quick shower, searched quickly for clean clothes, and run out the door.

Haidji

The fourth Game day started with the beautiful Hostess sliding over the stadium platform, wearing her Alexander McQueen Shoes and beautiful Dolce&Gabbana 'Femme Fatale' red dress, welcoming the public.

The first group of candidates came to the platform, already prepared for the game. It was the fourth day of jumping, the last day of the first step in the game before the day off, after which the second step of the Game would start.

Her voice overrode the combined voices of the bet sellers, the mob in the stadium, the Suicide Game t-shirt and souvenir sellers on the streets around, and the voices of the Hare Krishna group (who seemed to be murmuring a new mantra...'we all gonna'...'we all gonna...')

'Welcome to the last day of the first game step, thank you all for being here; at home, on the streets outside the Stadium, at your workplace, or wherever you are now, thanks for being here with me! Today I have 2000 more candidates, who will jump for you... and the first group is ready! Waiting for the signal. Let the countdown begin!'

And the counter started at 50, as she continued to speak.

'Live from the Night Stadium, especially for you, the last day of this first step, for you, the new and unexpected

SUICIDE GAME!

The new game
The new mania
8000 candidates and
Only one will survive
Only one can win!
Live from the Night Stadium
Nothing compares to what you'll see here
Nothing compares to what you'll watch
You have already chosen your candidate,

You have Made your bet

To be part of a

New and unexpected game

Now it's time to let all be in the laps of the gods

And when the bell rings...it is time to jump for your life!
10...9...8...7...6...5...4...3...2...1!

And the jump bell rang out loudly

JUMP!'

And the first group jumped...

Haidji

Cassandra was doing the makeup on the second group of the day. There were five makeup teams, each with two persons, each team to take care of forty candidates in a group, which made twenty candidates for each makeup artist.

Cassandra could swear that she made only nineteen, because she finished earlier than John, and this wasn't usual. As she finished the makeup of her share of this second group, John was only just starting to take care of his last candidate from this second group.

She walked around for a few minutes wondering how she could have been so fast; but better was to count the candidates next time, so she could be sure.

The candidates went down to the elevators as the platform was rising with the winners of the last jump. The same elevators that carried the mini-vans that carried the losers' bodies brought the next group of candidates to the ground to enter the platform.

Working on her next group, Cassandra counted the persons she needed to make up; 20, it was right, but she wasn't faster than John. Did she have one candidate less in the last group? Were the other makeup teams stealing candidates?

She asked John about it.

'No Cassandra', said John. 'The other teams steal only our work tools, because we are the best, they wouldn't steal candidates. Don't overreact! You probably miscounted. If they would like to prejudice us they would send us one candidate more, not steal one from us. Use your brain, girl!'

6

The Hostess' voice announced the second group of this day.

'Wow, the first group was great! Can the second group be better? They are all special! Watch with me! Are you ready? They are ready! Watch the counter...start at 50...and now...

Live from the Night Stadium, especially for you, the last day of this first step, for you, now the unexpected

SUICIDE GAME!

The new game
The new mania
8000 candidates and
Only one will survive
Only one can win!

Live from the Night Stadium
Nothing compares to what you'll see here
Nothing compares to what you'll watch
You have already chosen your candidate,

You have Made your bet

To be part of a

New and unexpected game

Now it's time to let all be in the laps of the gods

And when the bell rings...it is time to jump for your life!
10...9...8...7...6...5...4...3...2...1!

And the jump bell rang out loudly

JUMP!'

In the second group of the day, some candidates were missing. Number 6253 was one of the pregnant ones and was already sent home, but nobody noticed that were only 199 instead of 200 in the group that jumped. The same happened in the sixth, the last of the day's group; 7011 and 7821 were also sent home.

But the crowd did not notice.

It was a stressful day also for the workers who removed the dead bodies from the sandy ground; they needed to bring more sand quickly and spread it over the now too many blood spots. It was good that the next day was a day off, because they also needed to do some repair work on the Stadium itself.

G

Only 688 survivors, on this fourth day. The Council was wondering why. It should have been more.

Cassandra was speaking with other makeup teams, and two others also had the impression that they had been faster in some groups, or maybe missed a candidate? Maybe they were just tired, and miscounted the candidates.

G

The beautiful Hostess proclaimed the end of the fourth day, with a new surprise...

'I have a surprise for you! In one of the days of the next step, the winning group from the Facebook song contest organized by the teenagers, will sing live in the Stadium, before the Game starts! Yes, Life in a Wire will be here to sing for you! Rest tomorrow and enjoy your day, because you will need your rest, the second step is even better than the first one. More adrenaline, more surprises waiting here for you! Thank you for being here with me! Wherever you are, I will be here! Waiting for you, to show you...the second step of the Suicide Game!'

Life in a Wire's video on YouTube already had over 1 million views. Their song 'Suicide Game' was the new hit...and it had also increased the SG t-shirts sales, now available not only at the Stadium, but also online.

6

Cassandra stopped quickly at Alessandra's place.

To see how they were. They started to become real friends. In the middle of this weird game of life and death, she would stop there for a coffee, before she went to her work at the condominium. The small room, with the small garden, seemed like an oasis in the middle of the desert of the Stadium.

She asked Alessandra how she could keep the flowers in such good shape; her own flowers at home were always looking as would they prefer to be in the park across from her apartment on the other side of the street. Away from her.

Alessandra answered:

'The flowers, I don't know when they are thirsty; sometimes they drink a lot, other times the water stays and rots. Attracts insects and worms. You need to know them in their individuality, to know what they need. What they like, what they want from life. Sometimes I just follow my intuition and see if their leaves are bright or faded, like we make with human faces'.

Alessandra was still wondering where the baby came from; it was still a mystery for her and would maybe forever be a mystery. So, it was better not to speak to Cassandra about it, because she had no bracelet and the baby's one was deactivated or broken, and they could not go out of there until the end of the game. Some stadium rules could not be broken.

All the workers already knew the girl and the baby, and thought that the baby was her own child; she was, probably, a lover of a married man, taking care alone of the fruit of the sin, hiding herself inside the Stadium, while a complicated divorce was happening.

Maybe a child of a higher member of the Stadium staff? Too much TV series' in their minds, persons like to color life a little bit with gray tones, to make some shadows on it and make it more interesting.

If she would tell them that she had found the baby, they would think that she lied, and they would make her a kidnapper; so, the best was to be quiet and accept the rumors.

Don't speak about it, but don't deny it. The truth was too simple to be accepted. Nobody can just find a baby. She saw it as a kind of small miracle. And nobody understands miracles; they are mostly too simple to be understood.

Some of the workers felt friendship and compassion to her, poor young sinner, probably already regretting all she did...poor girl.... So they would bring them groceries, baby food and stop there for a small talk, before going off to their work. And maybe because it was good to see life, life starting in the middle of so much...dead stuff.

Cassandra rushed into work in the condominium kitchen. Because the next day would be a day off, they needed to prepare more meals for the candidates.

This night, Cassandra was so tired, so overwhelmed, that she started to feel worried about her candidate, who seemed, like all other candidates, not really aware of where he was, or what was going on around him.

As Cassandra finally reached her apartment that night, she was so exhausted and tired, so overwhelmed, that she needed a Red Bull, to calm down and fall asleep.

Chapter 12

Candidate 5151 – Bianca White

Bianca was around 20 years old, average size, blue eyes, and kind of shy sometimes, long golden brown hair.

She was beautiful, but she didn't notice.

She was sad, but she never showed it.

She was the kind of sad beauty that attracts persons as would they feel the need to take care of her, or the need to attack or take advantage of her innocence and ingenuity. Because the pureness inside her heart, would never break, no matter what could happen in her life.

She was the first to appear at a party, and the last to leave it, and she was always invited.

Her preferred quotes included: 'It wasn't Aristotle that said *Ces't la vie, Carpe Diem, Veni Vidi Vici*, let's do it! *Alea iacta est*!!! No, it wasn't!' ...And she would laugh loudly...'It wasn't! It was I!! Let's jump into it!!!'

The present moment is the combination of future and past...so let's live now and sometimes, sometimes let's just forget about the rest!

Philosophers must have turned over inside their coffins by laughter or anger, because of the way she used their quotes, adding her own words, and creating new meanings and points of views about it.

'Let's live restless! Life is a tour! Enjoy your day, rest a little bit, and start again! Also in a restless life, you need a day off sometimes...'

She never drank anything alcoholic, and she was far away from drugs; so then, she was adorable exactly as she was.

Sometimes she liked to be a little bit crazy, in order not to get one hundred percent mad.

And she loved to dance...

This is how she should be, how she was outside and also in the image she saw of herself in the mirror of her dreams, and she lived intensely. Because being one hundred percent in the present moment, she could avoid thinking about the past or future and could keep her real self and all her pain away from all and everything around her. But not away from herself. She lived with her pain.

It was a Sunday and Bianca woke up and realized that it wasn't a dream.

He really died. And now, she could speak about it.

It was a death like many other persons used to have in his generation, after a life with cigarettes and alcohol; he died because he did not have lungs anymore.

His lungs turned black, but his heart and soul were still at this moment darker than his lungs. His suffering wasn't a consequence of his sins, but a natural consequence of the way he treated his own body.

Contrary to the way that her family used to think about it, a disease doesn't choose between good and bad persons, to catch them.

But now, it was too late to speak about it, because as the last action in his life, he died; but he took all of them, in a certain way, with him.

They were not interested anymore to hear her voice about the past, and there were no embraces, just offenses. It was a slap in her heart. And they would never, never understand what happened to her.

They all forgave him; they not only forgave him, they also sanctified him. All his sins were forgiven, merely because he suffered for two months in a hospital bed.

'It was his past, his child traumas, alcohol'; they even mentioned 'bad spirits around him that pursued him in his acts'. Mother and sisters had turned into strangers, for Bianca.

She did not suffer with his death, but she wasn't happy about it; maybe she was a little bit relieved. And she remembered suddenly things that were locked inside her heart and even her memory for many years. He already abused her, as she was a small kid. Suddenly she remembered that. But once more, in her family, when you don't speak about things, it was as if they would never exist. They didn't want her to speak about it.

They suffered with his death and she—she suffered with their reaction to it.

All was unfounded.

He wasn't a father. He was a psychopathic monster.

What about all we learn, about to be a correct person, if someone can be bad all lifelong and come to heaven, after suffering only two months? What about the good persons who suffer the two months too, and then die from the same disease? Where do they go? Does heaven have different sections? Nobody answered her this question.

And now, she felt like a transparent shadow of herself. As would she be less than the air they use to breathe.

Made from another material. Fluctuating over the ground of reality.

He died and took all their hearts with him.

Bianca would step by step, or maybe even suddenly, disappear from their lives, because her presence would always remind them of how evil he really was while he was alive, and nobody wanted that. They wanted a new star at the Christmas tree to pray to. They wanted a fake angel or a fake saint; so let's let them have what they want.

Nobody wants to recognize evil when it is at his or her own house, and not at the neighbor's one.

He lived like a demon and died like a saint.

And he left his Sin inside her heart.

Because we all have a Sin somewhere, and if we don't, someone else will put a Sin inside our heart, so that we also have one.

So she said...ok...it is like it is.

Let's dance through life like a transparent shadow until exhaustion and then, fall into the arms of destiny.

C'est la vie, Carpe Diem, Veni Vidi Vici, Let's do it? Alea iacta est!! Let's jump into it!!!

Bianca decided to jump into the Suicide Game.

Chapter 13

The sun was still wandering through other countries and the lights in the conference room at the Stadium were already on, like a pale moonlight over the round white table.

Alphabot had already left the room, and the six coffee cups were already empty.

The voice of the Green council member echoed in the room, elevated over the night sounds.

Apart from the seven council members, and Alphabot, everyone was still sleeping.

'It is a day off for all candidates and most workers, but it is a day of double work for us; tomorrow the second step starts. And there is a lot to decide and modify before it.'

'How many had survived?' Asked Blue, as would he be speaking to himself. Let's see it. And he answered his own question.

'From the initial 8000 candidates, there were now 3640, already discounting the pregnant women...3640...what happened? Shouldn't it be 4000?

Someone needed to watch the Gravedigger more closely...did some of the wires really get broken by themselves? The initial idea was 1000 candidates a day on the second step, and now the number was broken...Mathematics should be perfect science...so should our administration of the game be.

And candidate number 7777 died, and this wasn't supposed to happen! Due to the research they made before, the most chosen numbers were 1234, 1111, and then 2222, 3333, 4444, and so on. Followed by birthday dates. And so they were keeping the most chosen numbers for the other game steps. What is going on there?'

Silence. They requested Alphabot to bring them more coffee.

Alphabot brought the coffee and Black said, before he could ask him:

'No coffee...no water...thanks.'

And the Green council member was wandering around the room...upset.

This kind of mistake could not happen again.

Could not happen again! Agreed Purple.

Yellow and Red also agreed.

Blue just said, 'maybe all is always in the laps of the gods and we don't have so much control about destiny as we believe we have; luck also has its percentage in the destiny of situations, no matter how much we work on it', and he smiled. 'But we shall watch the Gravedigger work more closely; maybe he is not working properly'.

They scheduled another meeting to speak about this issue again. Black, Purple, Green, Blue, Red, Yellow and White left the room. Alphabot came to close the door.

6

Not far away from there, at the Stadium, the excavators and trucks from a construction company arrived, together with Steven Laurence, who would never allow changes in his masterpiece without his permission and presence.

The ground should be now almost one meter deeper to allow two more rows of seats. And this isn't so simple, like it seemed to be when the depth was to be less than one meter deeper.

Ramps now needed to be made for the transport of the bodies out of the sandy ground.

Steven Laurence did not like the idea of 'ramps'. He did not like the idea of any change in his masterpiece, but a six-figure check that his friend White handled with him in person, together with compliments about his masterpiece, convinced him to let them excavate the Stadium ground. Did not take away his bad mood, but convinced him. And he then convinced the workers to excavate all the ground, making the corridors inside the Stadium and the rooms, also deeper...because he really did not like the idea of ramps...

As the new seats arrived, and also more gray sand for the ground, there were still workers working in the inside of the Stadium, and inside the rooms and corridors, because Steven Laurence could live with a higher roof, and he could change the size of all the doors, and he could excavate everything deeper into the Earth... but he could not live with ramps, which to him, were slides.

His masterpiece was made for serious games, it wasn't a kids' playground to have *slides*.

So, in the end they needed only 45cm more depth to set one new row of seats, the best seats...in black, shiny black. They made one meter of new excavation, to allow for the two new rows of seats and to accommodate a higher quantity of sand, to cover the ground.

And the ushers, after a discussion about who should clean the blood spots after the jumps, decided to just put new sand over always, it was faster and more practical this way. Had always been a problem to clean it all up so fast and properly.

Inside the Stadium a man wearing a Red Cross uniform was speaking to Demir, the chief of the ushers. The name of the man was Albion and he couldn't find the baby, the baby just disappeared. He brought the baby to the Stadium a few days ago to show it to Demir, his friend who was also one of the heads of the organ mafia, because Demir's cousin wanted to buy a baby. Not because of the organs, of course, but because his cousin's wife couldn't have kids, and they wanted one.

Babies came from catastrophes or even accidents. Wearing fake but well made Red Cross uniforms, Albion's crew was one of the first groups that appeared to help by an Earthquake, floods, fire, or even war.

They were a special unit, he said, mostly the first that would appear on catastrophes.

Of course they helped, but the main mission of his group was to find kids under two years old, especially babies, save them and sell them; it was the best business ever, because no one would ever miss or search for them.

It was better than his grandfather's and father's business in the 1980's, they were just kidnappers. Albion's family was proud of him.

Now he brought this baby, fresh from an accident in the UK, to show to his friend Demir; but the baby disappeared. He searched for the baby inside the Stadium and couldn't find it, and no baby came out, it must just have fallen somewhere and be already under the gray sand of the Stadium ground.

Albion went to the main office and asked to deactivate the baby's bracelet. He said that the baby was already gone before him and he wanted to deactivate the bracelet, just to not have the risk of his wife bringing the baby to the Stadium without him. And he waited awhile inside the entrance; nobody tried to come out with the baby.... Must have fallen in the sand. What a shame! Was such a beautiful one. Escape from an accident, to die in a game.

Albion reported all this to his friend Demir and promised to bring another baby for Demir's cousin in one of the next days. Or after the game, if his friend would stay some more days around. A similar one, of course.

Haidji

Demir was back from a meeting with Black, his contact and friend in the Council. Black should know that Demir always reads the list of candidates that left the game, and the list of survivors, and he counted everybody and between day 3 and 4...he missed 12 candidates, 12 good healthy girls, where were they? Did someone steal their bodies? Was it one of the ushers? Demir was sure that someone changed the lists from the days before, because he made copies...and now, was different.

Imagining the worst things that could happen, like one of his own crew stealing his beautiful bodies, he came out of the meeting with Black in a better mood.

Black was friendly, but also cold, direct, and sometimes he used to repeat sentences. Demir suspected that Black had Asperger's syndrome, but he never asked Black about it. It would be unfriendly and they were not that close. Anyway, Black explained, twelve women were pregnant and we sent them home. Pregnant women cannot be game candidates. Candidates number 4957, 7821, 3287, 5432, 1452, 1473, 0061, 2982, 7011, 6253, 4216, 1045 dropped out of the game, in a different way. 'Pregnant women cannot be...game candidates.'

Demir accepted the explanation.

It was good for Albion, that he saw Demir now and not before his meeting with the Council.

Pregnant women sent home wasn't good for Demir's business, but it was better than if someone he trusted would steal his daily bread, and he was happy about a new client, the firm of doctors who were into bioengineering.

So, Demir would stay some days longer to meet the new client, and could therefore forgive his friend Albion for losing the baby.

'Was just one baby more, added to the pregnant girls.' Demir laughed, it was a joke. 'Just bring me a new one, maybe a better one and don't lose it, we have enough accidents here everyday with the game candidates!' and he laughed again.

While the conversation between Demir and Albion was happening and the work was being made on the Stadium, with workers excavating the ground for the two new rows of chairs...inside the Condominium, they were excavating two steps deeper inside the candidate's minds...

Haidji

Chapter 14

Candidate 7195 – The Scientist

Was his name important? Persons called him 'The Scientist', not that he was one.

But he looked like one, or maybe he was one, inside his mind and soul.

He had one idea, between so many ideas, he had a big one, and sometimes he felt dizzy when he remembered that the world turned against the clock. A bizarre, but true, reality, which no one (so it seemed) really understood.

That not even the Earth was two times at the same place, because the Universe moves, the Galaxy moves, the Solar System moves...and one year later...we are never at the same place we were one year ago, time is a spiral and there are many spirals inside, and outside, the circles of life. There is, somewhere, a jump, which changes the energy, to more or less, depending on the energy of the Moment inside which we live.

But this, exactly this, together with everything else he had studied, including the Coriolis effect, the centrifugal forces and centripetal forces, gave him the idea...so easy and so simple.

Artificial gravity on one hand, levitation on the stand point and...on the other hand...it that was all part of his invention...the prototype was almost ready, and the vehicle...would work.

All he needed was some energy to start. It could be electric, gas, oil, petrol, coal, just some energy to start the engine, and the same energy that he understood, the energy that causes the jump, would do the rest.

But...then, suddenly, he started to think...and now what?

Would this change the world too much? His idea was to make a vehicle, a kind of new car, that could run on this energy – that he had found a way to harvest – endlessly, and it would be better for the environment, it seemed so good, but it had now turned dangerous, so suddenly...

How many persons could lose their work? How many companies could break?

Why do changes happen so suddenly in life?

His idea had come suddenly; was developed slowly with hard work and now, the final product was there...he had tested it alone, smiling about it as some kids saw it, thinking that it was a balloon or some...new kind of flight machine, flying car, maybe a military one...because he had to disguise its true purpose, so it could not look like a car.

Haidji

No, he was just a scientist, testing a prototype device that nobody could easily identify.

Where have we gone, he wondered? Are we so far gone, that something that could be good for the environment could be bad for the human race? Are we so far away from nature, so far away from the sky, so far away from it all? And yet, on the one hand, not even close to hell, but on the other, descending into hell, perhaps.

In a world where we don't need to create androids, because some of us seem to have been born without a soul, he still had one, at least for now.

So now he was there, paralyzed. The prototype was in the garage; plans, drawings and related things were around, over, under, and inside, the desk. And the cigarette lighter was in his hand. He was paralyzed, which is what happens sometimes when reality touches a dream and you realize that the world outside, which was already there and had inspired your dream, the world outside suddenly makes your dream seem like a nightmare.

He was confused, his idea had seemed to be so good, but maybe it was the worst one he ever had, maybe he should go back and make paper again, his special paper, made by cork rests and recycled paper. It was a good idea, but cork and paper companies don't like to work together in the same project.

After one month working day and night on it, a cork allergy, and a couple of meetings where they loved the paper (asking for his formula), the Scientist gave up, after hearing that the paper would only be made if he could, himself, convince the paper company to work with the cork one. Because, being different companies in the same city, they were enemies.

He destroyed the prototype.

He burned or smashed all his plans and drawings. Including other plans and ideas. While doing this, his study about the wind body fell out the window, being carried by the wind itself. (A boy found it on the street, picked it up and tried to read the plans, walking on the street going to drink his coffee at Starbucks. He didn't understand them and left the papers over the table as he went out of the place.)

It soon became clear to the Scientist that this didn't help much; he had destroyed the plans, but the idea kept going in circles inside his mind. But there were not many mind readers in the world; so, until he could decide if it was a good or a bad one...at least it was stopped. It seemed that everything all around and inside of him was paralyzed.

He started thinking of his ideas, and research, which had been reflected in the prototype, drawings and plans he had just destroyed.

Where was exactly the point where the Earth makes the 'jump'? Between one and another year?

It wasn't at midnight of the 31st December. He had figured it out, and how to harness the energy of the jump. This is probably the only thing he was sure about at this moment in his life; all the rest, in his life, was paralyzed.

The Earth's rotation was slowing down, a day was longer than it was 100 years ago; also when a sidereal day was almost 4 minutes shorter than a solar one, the Earth needed these almost 4 minutes to make a new solar day...this was his inspiration to calculate and understand the jump...and to find the answer to how his idea would work; just further observation and calculation had been needed.

The key to the answer wasn't in the equinox, but more in the perihelion and aphelion; anyway, the Earth wasn't at the same place it was one year ago, and he also not, and between North, South, East and West, he had the right answer, and he was going to help to make the world a better place with it.

But now, if this was the right answer, he did not know if it would still make a better world, or bring more confusion and war, or other forms of destruction, at first, before it would then help save the world. What is the cost / benefit equation here, he thought?

This increased his mental paralysis, to take the right decision about his idea, his solution, which he had just destroyed. Destroyed in his papers and plans, but not inside his mind and heart.

Because now, instead of thinking only about his idea, the cosmic jump, he was thinking about his own one also.

He could destroy the papers, but his mind was always awake, thinking about things. Maybe he could silence all inside of him with a jump. The world wasn't ready. He wasn't ready to fight longer. Everywhere he showed his ideas, persons denied them.

Suddenly, as he heard the bell inside of him, he decided...to jump into the Suicide Game.

It was time to forget about all his dreams, and jump into the unknown place named death.

Chapter 15

Inside the Condominium it was time for new seminars...this is how the candidates' day off was going to be...it wasn't a day off work at all, it was just a day off death, where none of them would die.

All candidates moved into their new rooms, after surviving the first step of the game.

Their belongings were left in their old rooms and transferred into small cabinets, where only special VIP guests could come and see if there were some things interesting, to be put aside in case they would die. The VIP's could buy them, before they sent the rest for charity purposes. And most of the time, the rest wouldn't be much, just enough.

Their new rooms were on the second floor of the modern condominium, all made of concrete, wood and green glass. No curtains on the windows.

They now used the 'Suicide Game uniform' version in sport clothes, to feel more comfortable; and, because a paparazzi was able to take a photo of them, the t-shirt sellers in front of the stadium started to sell also the Suicide Game sport pants, rain jackets, and socks.

Probably the audience would be completely dressed in SG couture on the next step in the game, because a complete outfit kit…was cheaper than two t-shirts.

The candidates woke up at 6am, by alarm. They went down to the seminar in the meditation room.

'Breath deep, relax… feel the calmness around you.

And now…imagine death. What do you see? Is it scary? And dark? Follow the steps:

Reduce the image in your mind.

Put some color into it.

Think about a calm safe place. A beautiful lake.

A beautiful lake with transparent water, there is safety, there is peace.

Inside the water…'

(And some candidates trembled, because they still saw dirty water and danger, even after many days of meditation…)

'The water is clean, believe in me.

Repeat to yourself, the water is clean,

The water is clean, the water is clean,

Water is the symbol of life

Water is the symbol of life

Water is the symbol of life

The world is what I want it to be,

The world is what I want it to be,

The world is what I want it to be,

Human beings have the gift of creation, and you create the reality you live in,

Create your own world. Jump into it...

Because reality is an illusion, the truth, the real truth is your wish, and you can change the world around you, with a simple jump into your dreams. JUMP!

The lake is deep and there is peace and happiness.

And only if you jump into the lake of your fears, you can survive.

Be focused, and concentrate, pay attention.

And when the bell rings...it is time to jump for your life!

10...9...8...7...6...5...4...3...2...1!

JUMP!'

And they all jumped into a swimming pool inside the meditation room. Dressed with their sports outfits. The water was warm and wasn't deep.

As they came out of the pool, the models were there.

Like angels dressed in blue, bringing with them breakfast trays, towels, fresh clothes and drinks.

And they felt great enjoying their breakfast.

As they were there, feeling great, they could hear the bell again and a voice whispering...

'Jump! 10...9...8...7...6...5...4...3...2...1

Jump! Jump!'

Like an echo...Jump...Jump...Jump, inside their minds.

$$\mathsf{G}$$

Then it was time for meditation on the grass, and then another seminar.

The day passed by very fast, because all that they did was already turned into routine, a routine they made every day since the first day in the condominium. Before leaving to go to the stadium.

But this was the day off, so instead of one seminar in the early morning, they had three. And then the last one, after dinner.

And they were all, more or less, confident; and all them were ready for the second step of the game.

Haidji

Chapter 16

The Gravedigger

He was small, not skinny, not fat, but small and his face was even ruder than his hands. Antonio was a Gravedigger in southern Spain, like his father had been, and his grandfather too. It was a kind of family business. The funeral agency belonged to his brother and his aunties were often hired as 'carpideiras', professional women to cry in a funeral.

But after years working (not officially) with a friend in the Alentejo region in Portugal, his family discovered that apart of being an honored gravedigger, he was involved in a scandal selling defunct bodies from Portuguese cemeteries to Spanish wizards for black magic.

If there would be a single Spanish skeleton involved, he would be found in one of the graves he was preparing for the next funeral, inside a black coffin.

But after a family meeting, with the 'carpideiras' crying and screaming—even without payment—his family, considering that all skeletons he sold were just Portuguese, decided to take him out of the business. A cousin was now working as an usher in the Suicide Game, and contacted him for a new opportunity.

They did not need more ushers, but he got the job to spend the night taking care of the gloves and wires, in a depositary room.

He spent the night there, bored already on his first work night.

The gloves were organized inside of shelves, with the wires already attached to them, in different heights on the shelving.

With his 1.45m height, the Gravedigger could only reach more or less half of the gloves and wires in the room.

Walking bored around the room, he found a toolbox; maybe one of the workers forgot it there.

He started to play with a hammer, making sounds and noise, playing with the hammer on the walls and floor.

But then he saw the orange wire cutter.

A sparkle went through his eyes, an evil sparkle.

He took the first glove, as would he cut the wire.

He couldn't cut it, but this made it fragile and for sure, this wire would break by the jump.

He took each one of the gloves and wires he could reach, and spent his nights damaging the wires.

On the fourth night, the night before the fourth day of the first step of the game, he was so fast that one hour before the end of his work shift, he had already damaged all wires he could reach.

He started to be bored again...and was trying to reach more gloves. He used the chair he was sitting in. He stood over the chair. And kept playing with the wire cutter, until the sound of the shift alarm, which told him that his work was done for this night.

Haidji

Chapter 17

Alphabot opened the conference room's door. Six cups of coffee were already on the table. White, Yellow, Red, Blue. Green, Purple and Black entered the room, sitting down at their fixed places, one after another.

The council held another meeting about the 3640 candidates. And now...? They would divide them through the four days and live with this issue, but someone needed to see what was going on with the Gravedigger—this kind of mistake could not happen again.

Was there not a security camera in the room where they deposited the gloves and wires?

Yes, there was, but no one has ever seen the images.

They saw the images and discovered what happened.

The Gravedigger damaged more wires than the ones he was supposed to damage.

They needed to make the gloves higher again. And find a solution for the problem.

There should be 1000/day to jump.

The better way to not have broken numbers, would then be to make 1000 on the 1st, 2nd and 3rd days, and 640 on the last day, suggested Purple.

But then Yellow suggested that it should be 640 on the first day, because there was also the new song, and other new things.

Green suggested that 640 should jump on the second day, just to suggest something.

'We'll vote about it…now', said Black.

But after voting four times, for which day should be the day with the lesser number of candidates, they decided it would be for day 3.

It was resolved: on the third day of the second step, they would have only 640 candidates. The third day was always the day with the least number of bets. It was therefore the best day for the fewer candidates.

Green wasn't happy, because his vote was 'no' for the third day. But he needed to live with the fact that the Gods never were on his side and seemed to be always on the side of the other members.

White and Black's answers seemed to be many times the accepted ones.

The Gods were always on the side of the same Council member; their chosen member, who practically chose himself, was not even sitting close to White on the round table; nor was he White himself. He touched his own metal sphere for a second.

The meeting was long, and finally, all decisions were made for this day.

Black, Purple, Green, Blue, Red, Yellow and White left the conference room in the Stadium, and Alphabot too, as the candidates were making their last meditation session for the day.

And it was in the 'laps of the gods', or better said, inside one of the metal spheres, and no more in the Gravedigger's hands, about how many of them would survive in this first day of the second step of the Game.

6

A white Labrador Retriever dog walked around outside the Stadium, between the vendors, public, Hare Krishnas and kid's parties' makeup artists.

Food trucks were there, selling all kind of fast or slow food, and the dog was hunting for real food, in a world where they had habituated him to dry pet food.

Smelling something different, the dog entered the Stadium and found the way to the gray sandy ground, and started to dig, searching for meat or bones.

Demir, the Usher chief, saw him and sent him away. Trying to escape from Demir, the dog ran around the elevator in circles and then went towards the outside of the grounds. And ended up in front of the room where the girl was living with the baby.

The baby was holding around itself, training to make its first steps...and suddenly started to walk alone into the dog's direction; as it saw the dog, speaking to the dog in baby language... 'Waw...waw.... waw.'

Now we have a dog, thought Alessandra; some days ago there was no money for the rent and now she had for some days a baby, a kind of small house with a little garden, and now a dog. Sometimes she felt happy and forgot the Stadium and the game around her, taking care of her small new family.

She embraced the dog, giving him some real food.

Alessandra called the baby Dawn.

And the dog Wow: because Dawn pointed to the dog saying 'waw waw', she decided to call it Wow. Because it was a really good surprise in her life, Dawn and Wow.

Her new small family.

Alessandra was teaching Dawn to say 'Wow', instead of 'waw', as Cassandra passed by to have a tea with her, after work.

Haidji

Chapter 18

Tim was between gigs, working at Starbucks, and often saw Tom and Clare, usual clients, coming to choose their morning coffee.

One morning Tom was drinking his coffee with Clare and, like many times over the last two years, he asked her again:

'Clare, why not? Why we don't try? You are single, me too, we are friends since years. Just one time, to see how it works, maybe I can surprise you, Clare.'

Clare laughed and answered:

'Tom, yes we've been friends for more or less two years, but I never felt attracted to you that way. And this will not change just because my ex-boyfriend recently married my ex-best friend.

For these two years we've been drinking coffee together sometimes in the morning, and I have to say that I've noticed, we never order the same coffee. Never. Never ever.

We don't even order each other's coffee on days when one of us gets here first. You are Mr. Venti Latte. Standard latte.

I could order for you without to speak, even Tim knows what you want; or why do you think that he smiles every time that you take 5 seconds to make your order, reading the list as would you chose, and then order *always* the same thing?

But you couldn't order for me even if you wanted to. Sometimes I want something straight up, like a Grande Americano. Sometimes I want something decadent like a Venti triple shot Caramel Macchiato, with extra whip. And sometimes I just leave it in the laps of the gods. I tell Tim to pick something and all I need to tell him is what cup size and my name, and he surprises me.

And we never even eat the same type of cake.

I think you should stop trying with me, and go have a cold shower and search for someone else to make your hormonal update.'

'Update Clare? You call it update?'

And she laughed. 'Yes Tom, update!'

'Search for someone else for your hormonal update Tom, I can be single now, but I am not available.'

And so, drinking his venti latte, Tom went from frustrated and upset, to happy. He had an idea for a new business. Based on Clare's words to him.

Update...Update!

�

Just around the corner, he opened his new business.

He invited Tim to the opening, and Clare too, of course.

Clare wasn't interested, but Tim filled in the Update forms.

And Tim, a hidden romantic guy, a little bit too shy to show his real personality, fell in love on his first 'update' some days after. He never called a woman 'princess' before, maybe it was her perfume? No, it wasn't; he knew it was her presence.

After 3 updates, he was completely out of his mind.

But after 3 updates, he would not have money for a next update, until the end of the month; it was expensive for him. He needed a second job. Urgently, since two weeks ago he couldn't go to Update. What if she would never be there again? What if she would change her preferences? Find another lover? Why had he not the courage to ask for her name? Phone number? The Update rules said, 'don't ask for personal details', but were rules not there to be broken? Now, he was paying the price for being such a nice guy.

His cousin, John, was working as a makeup artist at the Stadium for the Suicide Game. He told Tim they needed more makeup artists for the second and third game steps. Due the urgency of Tim's problem, John gave him some tips and general lessons. In exchange, Tim introduced John to another Starbucks employee, Jack, asking him to be the model for his makeup lessons.

John and Jack came closer.

Tim got the job, and started to work as makeup artist at the Suicide Game on the first day of the second step of the game, counting the days to be able to go to Update again and meet his princess.

It wasn't a 100% chance to see her again, but in his heart, this did not make a difference. He would do the possible and impossible. Tim had also tried to steal the database from the Update website, but his friend Louis, a computer hacker, was still in jail, so he couldn't do that for him.

Counting the days of future work, praying inside that she would meet him again, Tim started his job at the Suicide Game.

Chapter 19

Step 2 - Day 1

The Hostess walked over the platform again with her beautiful red dress; her voice and image came everywhere inside and outside the Stadium.

'Do you want something that lasts forever? Something like Love?

Do you already love your candidate? You made your bet; you were always on his or her side. But sometimes life takes things we love away from us.

But also sometimes there is still a chance, so small it is, to have our loved ones in a certain way forever present in our lives.

I have a present for you. A new chance to not lose your candidate forever.

To have him or her always with you.'

While she spoke, models entered the platform carrying a big model, wrapped in white shiny tissue.

The tissue burst into big flames of fire while she said:

'Just when you think that things are gone, a new chance comes.'

And the spotlight fell over the model.

Shiny. A big crystal model, a diamond.

'You were here, or at home, or in the Stadium; no matter where, you were already here with us on the first Step. Suffering for your candidate. Afraid by every jump, and relieved or happy after it. Winning or losing your bet, wining or losing your wish.'

The Hostess walked to the diamond.

'Now you don't need to break inside when your candidate dies, because you have a chance to be with him or her, until the end of your life, if you win the raffle.

And get...a Diamond.

Made from the ashes of your candidate, especially for you. To be worn on your finger, around your neck, or on your head as a tiara.

We have the best goldsmiths in the world working for us, if you need support to create your jewelry.

All you need to do, to have your candidate forever with you, is to...

Buy a raffle today. Because if he dies not today, tomorrow the raffle is more expensive.

And there can be only one diamond made for each candidate. Run into it.

In case your candidate survives and is the winner of the Game, and if you haven't won the raffle, don't feel sad. He will give you in person a real diamond, and a signed poster of himself, at the end of the Game.

To say thanks for your love and support of him, wanting him next to you, for your lifetime.'

The Stadium's spotlight fell again over the diamond model, while all the rest was dark.

The public had their lighters on, the SG kit was selling a lot, persons were wearing the T-shirts and fitness wear; and some even had the Game symbol on their foreheads, made by kid's parties makeup artists that used to work at kid's birthday parties. They came to the idea of having a spot in front of the Stadium and painting persons' foreheads like the candidates.

The Hostess announced also that in this second game step they would have five jumps per day. Two in the morning, two after lunchtime, and one in the evening.

Cassandra, John and Tim were in the same team of makeup artists. The number of candidates for each team to prepare was about the same, and there was more time between the jumps.

Five jumps a day, but the makeup took longer now; the Council ordered them to be more accurate.

There were complaints about somebody who saw a scar on a candidate's face on the first step. Good that they hired more personnel. Each team had more time to make the makeup of their candidates.

Only one makeup artists' team would work on the last game step, and the competition for that was getting harder. One of the teams was accused of attempting to destroy or hide another team's work tools. That team would be fired the next time that something would disappear, not only one of them, but the whole team. This solved the problem, for a while; no team wanted to be fired, they all wanted to stay there until the Game's end.

G

Cassandra was thinking about her last night's work in the kitchen. She had noticed that candidate number 3507...was allergic to the sauce; the sauce wasn't in his food.

And Candidate 2252 seemed to not notice her presence.

Watching candidate 3507, she noticed that sometimes he didn't seem to be so lifeless, like the other candidates.

He left the room one time, and his dinner also maybe wasn't usual.

She saw him picking up his mobile phone from his pocket, something really not usual for a game candidate.

Cassandra decided to take some of the sauce with her to see the allergic components. She was afraid that 2252 could also be allergic to something. Just for safety, she had written a line under the notice about the allergic candidate, saying that candidate 2252 was allergic to the sauce too.

Because she couldn't take the sauce with her, or even food, she dropped some sauce on her bra and brought the bra to a laboratory, in the next morning before work started.

The results would be forthcoming at lunchtime.

With Tim as the new element in their crew, they started to work.

The Hostess announced a new game day.

The platform went down to pick up the first candidates, and take away the diamond model.

And the first group, of this second step of the game, entered the platform.

Two hundred candidates in this first group in the first day of Step Two of the game.

But they started from the end of the row of candidates.

Unexpectedly, candidate number 0001 wasn't there.

Number 8000 was on the platform; the platform that was now, even though the public couldn't notice the change, fifty-one meters high, because of the two new rows of chairs. Candidate 0001 would jump on the last day of the second step of the Game; now they started with the last ones from the first step.

The countdown started at 50, while the Hostess, in her beautiful red Femme Fatale dress, announced:

'And now, live from the Night Stadium, especially for you,

SUICIDE GAME!

The new game
The new mania
8000 candidates at the beginning
Only 3640 left,
Only one will survive
Only one can win!

Live from the Night Stadium
Nothing compares to what you'll see here
Nothing compares to what you'll watch
You have already chosen your candidate,

You have Made your bet

To be part of a

New and unexpected game

Now it's time to let all be in the laps of the gods

And when the bell rings...it is time to jump for your life!
10...9...8...7...6...5...4...3...2...1!

And the jump bell rang out loudly

JUMP! '

Candidate 8000 died in the jump of this first group of the
first day of the second step of the Game.

The public did not expect that change in the numbers. Only
one girl had a raffle for his number...she would win a
diamond! She was excited about it, screaming, jumping out
of her seat.

While the survivors were celebrating with champagne glasses, the girl was in the audience looking at her finger, happy about it, that she would have a diamond...a diamond for her finger, without remembering that someone died for that.

The term blood diamond received a second meaning, in the second step of the Suicide Game. By cutting the diamond made from his ashes, part of her chosen candidate would go down the drain into the dirty sewer...but this was just a detail. Blinded by the diamond shine, she did not see that.

The second and the third groups to jump also created more happy faces in the audience. The fact that the girl had bought only one raffle ticket, and had won, increased the sales in an unexpected way; they sold more raffles for diamonds than betting tickets for survivors. And the yellow dressed bet sellers had more than double work to do, selling so many raffles for the diamonds. Because now, as the excited and happy face of the first winner was on all screens, diamonds were seen as the real deal inside the Stadium. Everybody wanted to be so happy like she was, keeping the shining part of the candidate around a finger, while the rest could go down the drain into the dirty sewer.

Haidji

Cassandra couldn't wait for lunchtime.

In one of her short breaks she called the laboratory. She told them that she went to a party and a friend dropped something onto her by mistake. She thought it might be drugs. She was worried about the friend and wanted to know what it was. 'It was vinegar', the voice on the phone said. And she breathed a sigh of relief.

But then the voice on the phone continued, 'vinegar, vinegar mixed with propofol...a drug also known as milk of amnesia'.

Cassandra was desperate, but needed to stay there and keep working until the end of her Stadium workday. Watching candidates jumping from the platform. Remembering and seeing the face of 2252, in each one of them.

At noon, seven persons from the crowd went, at the same time, to seven different washrooms. After 18 minutes, they went back to their seats.

This happened in the middle of a jump; disturbing the view of the persons they walked in front of, while leaving their seats, who complained loudly, screaming at them.

They did not liked to miss the jump, but they had to accomplish their obligation.

G

At the end of this day:

From 1000, only 432 candidates survived the day. And 568 persons went home happy about winning a diamond, which would be delivered to their home in a few months.

Chapter 20

Cassandra arrived at her work in the condominium a little bit earlier than usual. Her notice about the allergy to the sauce for 2252 had already been copied and posted in other places inside the kitchen. It was difficult to get a good job; persons didn't want to lose it.

She helped in the kitchen but was nervous and worried, letting things fall. As the candidates arrived for dinner, candidate 2252 was among them, but very awake. And he looked to Cassandra, as would he know her from somewhere.

She walked into him. He remembered her like out of a dream somewhere. Some red hair, a touch of a hand, and white, black and orange colors.

And nothing more.

She couldn't speak to him there. Like in a bar, she asked him to go to the male washroom. Meet her there. And there, in the middle of a washroom, he told her his story.

His name was Luca. Italian. He entered the game because he was upset and sad. More than sad and upset; his fiancée decided to marry his best friend Stefano. And this, after six years together.

He came back one day from a business trip and she told him. He did not find them together making love (which would be acceptable for his defense, in case he would murder the asshole).

No, she just told him, as casually as she would say, 'I'm going to the supermarket to buy some coffee, but instead of Lavazza, I prefer Segafredo'. As if it was so simple, like that.

'I will marry, but not you; now I prefer to marry Stefano'.

He started a discussion with her, and as the words finished falling out of his mouth like angry tears, he figured out that he couldn't hurt a woman. Then he started to scream and fight with Stefano, and from that fight he had the scar on his face. But...Lavazza or Segafredo were both Italian, so he wished both of them happiness in hell, and he decided to enter the Game...and die, because he was a coward, or maybe a good friend, because even angry, he couldn't kill his friend. But of course, Stefano got a scar too.

Luca's honor was broken. His heart too, equal to his honor.

To speak to Cassandra was for him like to wake up from a long dream. As would the pain about Chiara and Stefano be gone away.

No fiancée, no best friend anymore; now his stronger memory was some red hair and colors and now, she was there in front of him, and he asked her...Who are you?

Cassandra told him how they met.

And they made all the pieces together, about the Game.

Madonna Mia!!! Tomorrow...tomorrow he would jump again, and he doesn't want to die anymore...No! No! No!

He didn't want to die, or even jump.

Padre Pio!!!! His faith to Padre Pio would help him.

He needed to go back to the dining room, and they agreed to find a solution, to take him out of the condominium.

He called Cassandra, 'Il Mio Angelo di fuoco' and, as a good Italian guy, kissed her passionately before they left the washroom. And he promised to not eat anything that would taste like bitter vinegar, and to pretend to be lifeless like the other candidates.

Luca went out of the dining room, to the last seminar of the day, that was more like a dance class, hearing something like 'we all gonna die someday', in groups of two hundred, in circles dancing to the rhythm of the song.

Cassandra went home with her face more red than her hair, because of the kiss, and terrified because Luca would jump on the next day.

She did not know who Padre Pio was, or Madonna Mia, but she searched on the Internet; she saw all movies about Padre Pio's life and, if this would help, she would pray for him. While she was searching, and lighting candles, she had an idea to take Luca out of the game and out of the condominium.

She called John and asked him to bring some of his clothes to work the next day; for an unexpected visitor she would have at home, family stuff, someone was visiting her and missed the flight back, and needed something to dress for a day, while she could wash the dirty stuff... 'You know John, they come and think you run a hotel...a family hotel with Sheraton service...'

'Something else that your family visitor needs? Or just clothes...?'

'Just clothes, John', and Cassandra laughed. John was funny, and this made her relax for a while.

Haidji

Chapter 21

Step 2 - Day 2

We all gonna die

Someday

Some way

We all gonna die

Someway

Someday

One day on the subway

A man comes with a gun

He shoots you for your money

And then you're really done

And we all say goodbye

We all gonna die

Someday

Someway

We all gonna die

Someway

Someday

One day on the beach

You wanna make a swim

But a shark comes too fast

And in peace you need to rest

         And we all say good-bye

We all gonna die

Some day

Some way

We all gonna die

Some way

Some day

Don't wait for the day

Take your life, make your way

Jump into your destiny

And be part of history

         And we all say good-bye

We all gonna die

Some day

Some way

We all gonna die

Some way

Some day

Haidji

No matter how you die

Or what action you take

Since you're born

        Life is just a Suicide Game...

$\complement$

The public was out of their minds, with the performance of Life in a Wire.

One of the members of the group, three guys and one girl, had just turned 18 years old on this day, almost under-aged to be in the Suicide Game. It was also a good reason to wait until the second day in the second step, for their performance.

It was a group with different ages and styles, united by the love of music. Mike, an unemployed guy around 50; his son Gabe, who turned 18 this day; a girl Nathaly, almost 30; and David, a 40 year old ex-broker, were the components of Life in a Wire. They created their first song as a joke for the Facebook contest, but they had played together for years, every evening, in Mike's garage. Sending their CDs around the world, never getting an answer, they decided to make a video wearing the Suicide Game uniform, for the teenagers' competition. And there they were...as Winners.

While the group Life in a Wire was performing, the candidates were part of the live performance.

The candidates moved on the platform according to the beat of the song, in slow moves to the left and to the right. Then going on their knees at the last phrase of the song. Standing up as the song finished completely.

As Life in a Wire left the platform through the elevator, the candidates were like statues, waiting for the jump.

Two hundred candidates were ready to Jump.

Luca was one of the candidates.

6

Cassandra cried making Luca's makeup, in silence, tears sliding over her face, while Luca said to her:

'Mio Angelo di Fuoco, trust me, trust Padre Pio. I will not die, and if, and if I do, I will come back from the dead and pick you up to be with me, Angelo Mio. I will stand from the sandy grounds of the Stadium and fly into your arms. No wire will be between you and me.'

John and Tim did not notice what was going on, because they were busy with the makeup of their own candidates. Tim thinking about his princess, and John was in love, sending an SMS text to Jack in every possible break; none of them really awake to the situation around them.

Tim was doing the makeup of another candidate. It was a woman. As he saw her, she seemed so familiar that he trembled for an instant, as he touched her face for the first time; she looked at him, as would she be so far away but yet so familiar, so close to him.

Time stopped for a while...for Tim.

She was exactly as he would imagine his princess, if he could see her face out of Update. So beautiful, so kind, so fragile, and with a certain coldness as he saw her, coldness that disappeared as he touched her face. Like a layer of thin ice that breaks when you walk over it, suddenly.

With only a few minutes to finish his work, he tried to not imagine things; he was creating illusions, trying to find her everywhere, for sure she wasn't in this game.

And maybe she wasn't even in love with him.

But, who cares? He would go back to Update, until he found her again.

6

The voice of the Hostess announced the jump:

'SUICIDE GAME!

The new game
The new mania
8000 candidates at the beginning
Only one will survive
Only one can win!
Live from the Night Stadium
Nothing compares to what you'll see here
Nothing compares to what you'll watch
You have already chosen your candidate,

You have Made your bet

To be part of a

New and unexpected game

Now it's time to leave it all in the laps of the gods

And when the bell rings...it is time to jump...for your life!

10...9...8...7...6...5...4...3...2...1!

Haidji

JUMP!'

Luca tried to seem lifeless. He tried to be like a statue. He tried as hard as he could. But it wasn't hard enough. Luca screamed as he jumped.

Cassandra watched him in silence, screaming inside of herself, too. Luca's loud scream was like an echo in the whole Stadium. Hanging on the wire, screaming and laughing because he survived. As the platform touched the sandy ground, he realized that he should have been quieter.

Luca walked like a drunk to the celebration, walking over another surviving candidate. Thinking fast and moving his hands very quickly, while pretending to stumble and walk slow, Luca took his bracelet off and exchanged it with the other candidate's one.

Now, he was Candidate number 5508. Back in the condominium, he spent his day without eating, because everything tasted like bitter vinegar, and thanking Madonna Mia, Padre Pio and all saints, and even the Pope, for his good luck...for sending him his 'Angelo di Fuoco'.

323 candidates survived this second day, and Luca was one of them.

At the end of the day, the group Life in a Wire came back to sing again their 'Suicide Game' song...but without the candidates, who were already out of the game, or back in the condominium.

Haidji

Chapter 22

John was cranky. He wanted perfection.

But so many hours working, painting faces of strangers, with a kind of counter and scheduled time to do it.

He did not know the name of the persons, or more about them, it was like a marathon.

Where was his idealism? He felt sometimes like a doctor saving human lives, making the beauty of them come to shine, as would life be no more than an inside and outside beauty contest.

There was a time when he knew the name and story of each person he worked with.

But these apathetic candidates? Were like dolls, like puppets hanging on wires.

He wanted to be the perfect makeup artist! The best of all of them.

He spoke to the candidates, no words back.

He learned how to read their non-expressive faces, also with no words.

He learned to see in their expression marks, if they were happy or sad persons.

And he learned to read the words they spoke through the silence of their voices.

Speaking with the surface of their skin.

He started to speak to them with his makeup colors.

Became better than he could ever be before, while the small talk was part of his life.

With the silence of the candidates, painting his puppets (how he started to call them, in an affectionate way), John learned more than in all his life before. And became the master of all makeup artists.

By every jump he saw his puppets falling, wishing they would still be so beautiful, when they go to the sky.

It was their choice to jump and die. All that John could do was to make them beautiful, for the last moment in their lives.

ᘓ

Still working on his puppets, he told Cassandra that the bag with the clothes for her family problem was ready; she could take it with her. Oh My God!

Now he understood why she was late to work sometimes; family do sometimes think that we run a hotel with full service, just because we live in a real big city. Not even Bed and Breakfast, they expect full service, if she needs more than some clothes?

Cassandra said thanks for the clothes, and no, she did not need more, and she would bring the clothes back soon.

John did not need the clothes back, they were from last year's fashion, he wanted to give them away anyway, her parents could keep them.

'Out of fashion, out of his wardrobe', was one of his life rules; no unnecessary things at home, he did not have much space and needed to make more. 'Who knows? Maybe Jack would move in one day? You never know my dear, when loves comes and changes your life…'

Cassandra knew about Jack, but preferred to not speak about it, just smiled; and smiling, Cassandra took a decision. Not one day longer for Luca in the Game or condominium. She had an idea that could be done on this night.

Cassandra did not stop at Alessandra's this evening after work, so she arrived a little bit earlier in the condominium, saw Luca walking around, and made him a signal that meant that she was waiting for him in the washroom.

She crossed paths with candidate 3507, who was again on the phone inside the washroom. He went out, too fast for a candidate on drugs, as she entered. It was the male washroom. He did not ask her what she was doing there, just ran out, as would he have seen a ghost. She looked in the mirror, was she maybe too pale? Good that she had always some makeup available. So she made some more color in her face.

Luca entered the washroom; after a kiss and an embrace, Cassandra asked him for his bracelet, and told him her idea.

She gave him her own bracelet, which he put on his wrist, for him not to be without; and she put Luca's bracelet on her own wrist.

Once in the kitchen, working, she dropped the still cold meat sauce she took out of the fridge, by mistake over Maria, another kitchen workers, arm, wrist, bracelet and hand. Maria, so far as she knew, was vegetarian, she could support seeing others cooking meat, but to touch it herself, was too much for her. She worked in the kitchen because she really needed the money to keep her own vegetarian restaurant going, together with her sister.

Haidji

Maria was almost fainting, not because of the sauce that wasn't even warm, but because of touching the meat without gloves. There were just some drops over her bracelet. Cassandra had taken care where she dropped the sauce.

Cassandra apologized, and offered to clean the bracelet for her.

Pretending to clean the bracelet, while Maria was recovering from her shock, being held by other kitchen workers, Cassandra took Luca's bracelet off her wrist, put it under hot water, put Maria's bracelet on her own wrist, and gave Maria Luca's clean and now (due to hot water) deactivated bracelet.

As Cassandra brought the trays to the candidates, she gave Luca his new bracelet, which was Maria's one, and took her own one back.

Already hidden in the washroom was the bag with John's clothes, a little bit too tight for Luca's taste, but he could wear them. There was a paper with her address, her handwritten GPS coordinates, and a key.

Luca left the Stadium together with some of the workers. Nobody noticed him. He walked around a little bit and stopped at the small supermarket next to Cassandra's place, to ask where exactly the apartment was and to buy ingredients for fresh pasta.

Amazing globalization: around the corner is where you need to go to find everything and if not, someone delivers it to your home. He found everything he needed to make a real Italian dish. The supermarket couple smiled, it was the first time that a guy had asked for Cassandra's place. They looked at him from bottom to top and approved him. Italian? Some passion is good for her.

Relieved to be out of the Game, he enjoyed the peace in her apartment and started to cook dinner. Cooking was like meditation for him. No TV, no CDs, only the sound of wine falling inside his glass, the sound of food being made in the kitchen, and the usual street noise with the background sounds of birds in the park on the other side of the road, and a beautiful woman coming home soon...who needs more?

Finished with her work, Maria wanted to go out of the Condominium. She was explaining to the guard that she needed to clean the bracelet, and the water was probably too hot; it wasn't her fault if their technology wasn't prepared for something so simple like hot water.

She had a family waiting and couldn't lose time waiting for a new bracelet or the result of a DNA test to prove who she is. Or did he think that someone would copy her beautiful old woman figure and paste it onto another body, to work in a kitchen like a slave? He couldn't even recognize her from the day before...?

They should create something better next time...idiots! Something waterproof, for kitchen workers.

The guard was tired and it was getting late. He knew Maria from the other days. She should just go. He would give her a new bracelet on the next day; but now, Maria, just go. After a day working on the Condominium entrance, protecting all from the paparazzi, or fans trying to break in...he was tired. He didn't need more drama in his life.

AHG left the condominium early that morning, well before light, so he could try to return as early as possible. It was not supposed to be known that he could leave, or return. He would have a coffee with Marcel, and a meeting with his lead defense counsel in the Big Oil case. The meeting was to discuss any remaining details for the trial, which was fast approaching.

They met at a Starbucks, the only place open early enough that served good coffee. Or his preferred place anyway.

To his surprise, his journalist friend was late, but a girl was there to speak to him. She came to his table after asking one employee where he was. Marcel had told her to ask for 'Tony', the name on his cardboard coffee cup.

Diana introduced herself. She was many things, but she wasn't shy. She came to visit her brother Marcel for a few days. From Asia. Tony, or better, Anthony, a/k/a AHG, did not know that Marcel had a sister, but due to her beauty, he could understand why Marcel kept her hidden, protected and a secret from him. In the public view, he was a married man and Marcel was a kind of conservative, Anthony was conservative too, in a certain kind of way, he never really cheated on his wife, even when he knew about her personal trainer. He was always too deeply involved with his work.

Marcel would come in about 10 minutes, she said. They spoke about the business world in Asia. Anthony was impressed about her knowledge and practical view of things.

She wasn't only beautiful, she was intelligent too. Dangerously intelligent.

And these 10 minutes, were enough to make Anthony fall in love with Diana, with her short modern black hair and black eyes.

But most of all, he fell in love with her mind. He asked her to drink a coffee with him on another day. She accepted.

As Marcel finally arrived, Diana left. Anthony's lawyer arrived too. So they couldn't speak about the game. And Anthony couldn't ask about Diana, but she had given him her phone number. Feeling like a teenager, he tried to concentrate in his business meeting with his lawyer.

Over their first coffee, his lead counsel explained that he almost didn't make the flight back in time for their meeting. He had just returned from Europe, where he had represented some clients in a negotiation about stolen art works. And while Anthony needed a coffee to put Diana out of the first thought in his mind, his lead counsel needed a coffee first, too, to go from oil colors of Matisse, Renoir and Monet, to another kind of oil, into Big Oil, changing hues, inside the shadows of law.

And Marcel, he didn't really need a coffee, but drank one anyway.

The meeting was successful; even with the dirty oil colors from Big Oil, they could clear some points and prepare the next steps.

As Anthony came back to the condominium, it was already after lunchtime. He came in time to take part in the dance lessons for a new choreography, more frenetic than the last one.

Anthony liked the sound of the song. It was like himself, trying to not fall in love with the Diana; his heart was freaking out while his mind was trying to be concentrated in the Big Oil case. It was good to freak out for a while.

All of them would be part of the choreography, with or without the singers, but they needed to learn all the parts, as would the singer's group be with them; it was part of the group spirit.

Chapter 23

Step 2 - Day 3

Cassandra was late again; did she lose her sense for responsibility? John was upset, but Tim was there to help him now, Cassandra brought him and Tim a coffee from Starbucks, maybe it was the reason to be late, I forgive you Cassandra...you look so amazing today, as would you be the happiest woman in the world.'

And yes, Cassandra was happy. She had homemade pasta the night before. And all she said was:

'It's such a shame that we can't see the stars when the sun is in the sky...last night was a starry night.'

'Starry night, Cassandra? Do you have fever? In this city we don't have stars in the sky, they are all on TV!! In the sky we have only clouds and pollution. And lights...and flights. Helicopters... Ok, maybe one or another star...but starry night? You're really a city girl Cassandra, that sees a couple of stars between clouds and calls it...Starry night! One day you should travel to the desert or to the mountains...and see what a real starry sky is....'

Cassandra smiled. She didn't need to go to the desert to see stars, or put the TV on; it was a starry night. With or without lights, pollution, flights, or clouds in the sky.

For her it was a starry night.

6

The day started with Life in a Wire performing a new song.

The Hostess, beautiful as always, announced the group. And welcomed the public to the third day of the second step of the Game. Five Jumps, and the first group were on the platform, together with Life in a Wire.

Mike, Gabe, Nathaly and David started to perform. The song started with a slow movement...increasing second after second. The candidates were dancing on the edge of the platform, synchronized with the beat of the song. At first slow...then very fast, trembling and shaking, as would their bodies be a physical representation of an over accelerated heart beat.

Suicide Freak

We came here for a party
They promised us a dance
Unforgettable they said

Let's leave it all to chance

So music now let's play
We'll all kick ass, ok
'Cause things are not so bleak
Now we're all a Suicide Freak

About the Freak, they said
All black cool, from toe to head
Remember keep your rhythm
As all is getting dead

My life
Your death
All is just one breath

Your life
My death
All is just one breath

Our life
Our death
All is just one breath

Party on and die

Die and party on

Party die and party on

Says the Freak

As the song was ending, resonating everywhere, the platform went down and came up again with the first group, 128 candidates, and Life in a Wire. It was the 640 candidates day.

AHG was in this group. He had asked to be in the first group. To be back at the condominium early, hoping to escape for a coffee with Diana before dinnertime.

It was a frenetic choreography, starting slow with the candidates dancing to the song, the crowd standing up to dance with it. Even for the beautiful Hostess, it was difficult to keep her foot quiet on the platform, while the performance raged on.

The sound was loud and the Stadium itself seemed to be trembling with the song. Outside, persons were dancing in the street.

The Hostess spoke, walking over the platform, beautiful like always, and still moving with the beat of the song:

'And now, after this amazing song from Life in a Wire, we can all calm down and be ready to jump...the counter will start at 50...count with me, I count with you, to support the candidates because here, and now...

Live from the Night Stadium, especially for you, the counter already started and I welcome you to

SUICIDE GAME!

The new game
The new mania
8000 candidates at the beginning,

Many have already been dropped from the game
Only one will survive
Only one can win!
Live from the Night Stadium
Nothing compares to what you'll see here
Nothing compares to what you'll watch
You have already chosen your candidate,

You have Made your bet

To be part of a

New and unexpected game

Now it's time to let all be in the laps of the gods

And when the bell rings...it is time to jump for your life!'

She spoke as would she be the counter's voice.

The counter was showing its numbers on all screens inside and outside the Stadium, inside people's homes, and in their hands on mobile phones, or other devices.

'10...9...8...7...6...5...4...3...2...1!

And the jump bell rang out loudly

JUMP!'

They jumped, some candidates still shaking, as would they still be dancing the freak song, while they jumped off the platform.

AHG survived, of course. And went back to the condominium, in time to met Diana.

The second, third and fourth groups of the day also danced before jumping, accompanied only by the beat of the song.

Life in a Wire came back to the platform stage to sing again, with the fifth group.

Mike, Gabe, Nathaly and David performed their song live and the models exchanged their blue dresses for Suicide Game kits, to dance with them. They all fell down over the platform as the song ended, to the applause of the crowd.

The Hostess, walking between the models on the floor, in her beautiful Dolce&Gabbana Femme Fatale dress, announced the end of this day. The lights went off and the platform went down.

From the 640 candidates who jumped in this day, only 208 Suicide Freaks were alive at the end of the day.

The public was pleased with the new choreography. It was a new hit, for sure. Even after sundown, people were dancing in the streets around the Stadium, or inside their own living rooms.

Haidji

Chapter 24

The council was searching for candidate 5508 and couldn't find him. He wasn't among the dead or the survivors, but had simply disappeared. Can it be that someone had stolen his body?

Black went to the Stadium ground to speak to Demir, who was there speaking to his workers.

Black shook Demir's hand and asked him, 'have you seen candidate...5508? Somewhere among the dead ones...maybe? Have you seen candidate...5508?'

Demir said, 'No, I have not seen candidate 5508. I counted them all exactly, and 5508 has not been among the dropped candidates of the game. Maybe he fell too deep and is under the Stadium's gray sand. Sometimes they fall, as would the Stadium ground become iron after catching them, and it is not easy to take them out the sand. But I will look for him.'

'You will look for...him', said Black.

The other council members also asked around, but nobody could find or had seen the candidate 5508. They voted about it and accepted the version that he should be already buried under the Stadium's grey sand.

The actual 2252, who was the candidate Luca took the bracelet from and gave his own bracelet to, got an injection, because of the loud scream in the game—maybe the drug wasn't strong enough for him. While Luca, the real 2252, now with no number or bracelet at all, was at Cassandra's apartment, looking at the park outside.

Looking through the window into the park, he was thinking about his life, and almost death.

His decision to die brought him love and a new life.

He was happy that around the corner was the small supermarket in which he could find all he needed to make an Italian dish. But to stay at home doing nothing was something he couldn't support.

Out of the game, out of his own country, he stopped at the supermarket and found Lavazza and Segafredo; it made him smile; thinking about love, past and new life, he wasn't angry anymore.

He wanted to start this new life. But he couldn't just hang around all day.

Luca decided to write.

While Cassandra was working in the Game, he started to write. Inspired by his own life and experiences in the condominium, he started to write a book.

'The Backstage'.

Alphabot brought the second round of coffee to the meeting room. And Black said for the second time:

'No coffee, no water...thanks.'

The Gravedigger was still creating problems. The Stadium wasn't his cemetery; he couldn't just make what he wanted to do.

Things were getting out of hand, out control, screamed Red. Out of control!

The Purple council member suggested calling a friend of his, the Geek. Maybe he could come immediately. After 30 minutes and six more cups of coffee delivered by Alphabot, the Geek entered the room.

His name was Louis Rousseau, but everyone he worked with knew him as 'the Geek'.

Purple had gone himself to speak to Louis, who was out of jail again; he used to spend a half day or night there sometimes, between one or another deal.

Louis Rousseau, the Geek, had a new task.

A rush order from the Council. Delivered to him personally, in a secret meeting place, by Purple. Because of the importance and the urgency, he negotiated a stiff fee. He didn't need the money. Nobody would ever know he was already a millionaire several times over, at least. He was a real IT badass, but hardly anyone knew it. He liked it that way, being an IT wolf in a geek sheep's clothing.

These days, he worked only for the thrill of it. Keeping him sharp and hard. Inventing new mountains to climb. This was his motivation. But to his customers, who were mostly uncool, greedy opportunists, he would only offer his masterpieces dearly.

This new assignment was challenging, even for him; it was the only reason he accepted it. The hardware would be pretty simple, but the software would be very tricky. Purple had explained the Council's needs.

They wanted a system to control the candidates' wires, so they could reliably control who would die in their jumps in the Game.

The system needed to be secure from physical or electronic tampering of any kind; could only be accessed and controlled by specific persons designated by the Council; and, most important of all, the system would need to be totally immune to hackers.

The Geek set to work.

He quickly designed the system's basic architecture and sourced the components using his secret network, so nobody could link the components together and attempt any reverse engineering. A micro-laser inside each candidate's glove would, when commanded, immediately and silently cut the wire, in a nanosecond.

The command would come by wireless signal, sent by a transmitter at the edge of the platform. A wireless cloud-computing network, set up with next generation encryption, would control the system.

Only the Council's designees would have access. Passcodes would change at least 24 times per day. Multiple redundancies were built in, to make everything fail-safe.

For the Geek, this was all business as usual.

He reserved his signature moment for the wireless network part of the system. This was the challenging part. It would be totally unhackable.

He wrote the software code for it from scratch, every bit of it. Each packet in the streaming data transmission signal would be wrapped in a spinning cocoon of encryption.

Even if a hacker could intercept the signal and, given a miracle, break the encryption code within nanoseconds, the encryption cocoon would already change before the hacker could access the decoded information, let alone try to alter it. Even the Geek, himself, thought this was radically cool.

The system was ready. They decided to test it in the next game day.

'Would be a stormy and rainy day...let's make some improvements, and test the new stuff also', suggested Yellow.

'We'll vote about it...now,' said Black

They voted about it and the council agreed.

The Gravedigger wasn't a problem anymore.

Purple laughed, thinking about the modern new way.

The wireless way to cut wires.

Chapter 25

Step 2 – Day 4

The sky was falling all over the Stadium. Nobody expected such a tempest. As would the souls of the already dead be crying over the public, rain was falling, crying for the ones that were gone, and for the ones that stayed.

Steven Laurence was a genius. He had thought about rain. So, over the platform, a roof opened by the first sign of water. Transparent like glass. But it wasn't glass.

Covering the whole area, so the rainwater would not destroy the beautiful red femme fatale dress. The system would protect the Hostess, and the platform. For the crowd, he thought that the more inclement the conditions, the more visceral their experience would be—and after all, they were paying to live an unforgettable experience.

All he saw before was heavy, boring, old looking. He wanted to innovate, to have the right strength, flexibility, and transparency. He knew what he wanted; he wanted to be the new breath in Architecture. For this, it was simple; to be a new breath all he needed was

Air.

He called it 'Windplate'.

Inspired by a piece of paper he found one day lying on a table at Starbucks, something about a lost study that someone once made, about something called the 'wind body'. The study was very interesting, and the description clear into details; he discovered that it wasn't a simple pattern, and he made it.

It was elegant in its simplicity. The Stadium was round, with the platform in the center and the elevator in the center of the platform. This allowed the crowd a good view, regardless of their seat location.

Laurence created an invisible plate of wind, suspended above the platform. Emanating from the top of the elevator shaft, silent forces created a small wind circle about one meter thick, which could be controlled in diameter and strength to achieve the desired measure of protection.

The wind plate spun in circles over the platform.

No rain, dust, birds or bird droppings could ever fall down on the platform. Instead, the Windplate's centrifugal forces swept them all aside, to fall outside the platform area.

When he realized how truly innovative his 'Windplate' really was, he immediately filed a patent for this new wind energy instrument.

The crowd was surprised and wondering, looking between the candidates and the Windplate.

Trying to understand how, with no physical deck, the rain wasn't falling over the platform; as would the Storm itself cry around the candidates but with its tears falling only outside the platform's edge, where they, the crowd, were standing. Inside all was dry. They called it Magic.

The day's proceedings started, with the Hare Krishna group selling iPods, CDs and songs in front of the stadium. Nobody, apart from smokers, would buy lighters under the rain.

And the Hostess announced:

'Thank you for being here, under this terrible weather. Thank you very much for your support and attention, I hope that I, that we all, I mean ... almost all...survive this game day...you know what I mean, the counter already started, under the tempest, they are here, ready to jump for their lives.

A big round of applause please, for the candidates, welcome to

SUICIDE GAME!

The new game
The new mania
8000 candidates
1000 candidates today!
Only one will survive
Only one can win!
Live from the Night Stadium
Nothing compares to what you'll see here
Nothing compares to what you'll watch
You have already chosen your candidate,

You have Made your bet

To be part of a

New and unexpected game

Now it's time to leave it all in the laps of the gods

And when the bell rings...it is time to jump...for your life!

10...9...8...7...6...5...4...3...2...1!

JUMP!'

The first group jumped, under the rain.

6

Around lunchtime, the Hostess announced that there would be an extra jump this day, especially made for those in the crowd who had come, under storm and rain, to watch the Game.

And the good part was that it wouldn't be just an extra jump. Not only this day's candidates would jump, but all candidates; all survivors from the second game step, would jump together, at the end of this day. Probably over 1000 candidates, depending on how many would make it in this game day.

'Over 1000 candidates jumping together under the rain, just for you. This will be something really amazing! '

Minivans were already bringing the candidates from the condominium, and the makeup team artists were working with no breaks, to make all the 963 candidates from the other days ready for the last jump of this day.

With 125 winners from this fifth jump, added to the survivors from the other days of this second step, there would be exactly 1088 candidates for the extra jump.

G

The Gravedigger was also watching this last jump. He was curious about how many would die, because after his damaging of the wires, all candidates whose wires he damaged had died; but the 1088 had survived, so when they jump again, no wires will break...so it can only be a joke, this last jump. Maybe they wanted to make a big celebration with all 1088 candidates? There were probably not so many champagne glasses or models there; all this was strange, but worth to see, thought the Gravedigger.

It was time for the last jump of the day, the 'Extra Jump!' The platform was full with candidates and dancers, who were ex-models.

Two, three or sometimes even more candidates were now using the space that one candidate usually used. The platform was more than just full.

Rain was falling outside the platform. Due to the roof system, the Hostess was dry and beautiful.

But the candidates were at the outer edge of the platform, and raindrops were falling over them, sliding over their bodies as would they be washing their souls from all questions and doubts, before their jump into an uncertainty destiny.

Morris, the computer freak sitting at the main computer on the control room, was waiting to test the new wireless system. With all seven Council members, and Louis the Geek, standing directly behind him.

Step by step, even the Hostess could recognize the candidates. All dressed in the same way, same makeup.

But there was something impossible to change, under all the makeup.

And this something was their individuality.

Still alive inside of them, until their last moment.

Still visible even for the ushers, as they dragged the lifeless bodies through the sand on the ground.

Even then, they still were individuals.

With something unique, impossible to be changed.

The Hostess saw them so close to each other on the platform, and she liked the idea of the extra jump, but was also when the idea to see that they were individuals had started to disturb her. She did not have time to think, the countdown already started.

The voice of the Hostess was loud and beautiful.

'Now, live from the Night Stadium, especially for you,

For you that came all the way here under this tempest, for you in front of the Stadium trying to see something through the rain curtain, for you at home, or at work, being here with me under this terrible weather all day,

For all of you, the extra jump, to thank you for being here with us today, no matter where you are, thank you for being here with me, welcome to the extra jump, welcome to

SUICIDE GAME!

The new game
The new mania
Now only 1088
Only one will survive at the end.
Only one can win!
Live from the Night Stadium
Nothing compares to what you'll see here
Nothing compares to what you'll watch
You have already chosen your candidate,

You have Made your bet

To be part of a

New and unexpected game

Now it's time to let all be in the laps of the gods

And when the bell rings...it is time to jump for your life!

Haidji

She spoke in harmony with the countdown, with all screens showing her, together with the countdown numbers.

10...9...8...7...6...5...4...3...2...1!

And the jump bell rang out loudly

JUMP!'

They jumped, all at the same time, still hearing the echo of the bell's sounding, as the Hare Krishnas and teenagers were singing the new Life in a Wire song, Suicide Freak, outside and inside the Stadium.

And after the 21-meter free fall...Morris touched the computer screen. There was a 'click' sound, which no one could hear outside the control room.

The Geek and the seven Council members were standing behind Morris, watching the candidates on the computer screen.

It was, as if something had gone badly wrong.

Like a black mass. Falling out of the game, as a bolt of lightning crossed the sky.

Bumping into the Stadium ground, with a dumb drum thunder sound, where the wet sand embraced their bodies.

The Public stood up trying to see the ground. But they could see...nothing. Sand was in the air. Like a rare tempest in the desert, they felt embraced by the thirsty sand.

The Gravedigger was scared, and he wasn't easy to scare, he almost jumped after the candidates to see what was really going on, but stopped in the last second and went down with an elevator.

Are they all dead? Are they all dead? Are they all death?

Persons were screaming.

White mist came over everything; the oldest trick, dry ice. To create magic, or just to avoid the cameras showing the bloody ground of the Stadium.

The Ushers couldn't finish their work removing all the bodies, and didn't even have time to make the sand look fine again, or to remove all them, as the platform came down with just seven candidates hanging on their wires. The Gravedigger started to help them with the bodies.

The platform came slowly up again, all lights on the Stadium falling over it.

Where each one, with a champagne glass, was celebrating, and the beautiful Hostess was announcing the end of the four days of the Second Step:

'Here: the Seven Ultimate Candidates.

Yes, life takes unexpected ways sometimes.

From a huge possibility of choices at the beginning of this day, only seven were correct.

The next day will be a day off. But then, I will have a surprise for you in the third Step of the Game, thank you very much for being here with us today, under tempest, under rain, thank you for being here in the last day of this second step from Suicide Game. A big round of applause please, for the Seven Ultimate Candidates.'

While the crowd was clapping and whistling, the platform silently went down to the Stadium's sandy ground. The minivans were already there; ready to bring the candidates to the condominium.

They were not only the Seven Ultimate Candidates now.

They had turned into Celebrities.

They needed special bodyguards with motorbikes around the minivans, to escape from the paparazzi on their own motorbikes, on the way to the condominium.

Haidji

Chapter 26

Cassandra stopped after the game at Alessandra's, to see how she and the baby were doing by the storm, and asked if she might want to come over to visit while they were doing the makeup of the seven last candidates, the next morning. Alessandra would come with Dawn and Wow.

Only one makeup artist team would stay for the Third Step of the game, and this could only be the best one. Cassandra, John and Tim were in this best team; it was an honor. They were the best team. John was more than happy.

The other teams would now work outside the Stadium, because the kids' parties' makeup teams couldn't cover the demand for symbols to be painted on the public's foreheads. To have the real candidates makeup artists' teams outside, was a great idea, of course; voted and approved by the Council members, after being suggested by Blue. And, of course the makeup, made by the real Suicide Game makeup artist teams dressed in their real uniforms, would be more expensive.

Cassandra appeared to work in the kitchen, but as a part-time worker she was told to just help to clean the kitchen, then she could go home; with only seven candidates left, they wouldn't need her for the last game step.

Cassandra came home earlier, this night. And decided to walk with Luca in the park. For the first time since she moved into her apartment, she was in the park and she felt good there, walking hand in hand with Luca.

The other kitchen workers joined the group of workers that separated the losers' belongings. For the different charity groups and/or sellers.

The Council had directed that the seminars would be made individually, in the next day. So also that nobody could notice if Anthony wouldn't be there.

6

Alessandra was looking into Dawn's bright eyes and thinking. The baby walked after the dog, calling it wow wow, smiling and laughing after him.

Was good to see the baby's eyes. Most persons she saw before being inside the Stadium with Dawn and Wow, were wearing sunglasses.

Few were the persons whose eyes she could see. Most of them hid themselves behind sunglasses. As would masks not be enough anymore, in a world where a 20 year old was too old to be a model, but they expect persons to retire at almost 70, and die with 100.

What about persons who see work as...something to fulfill their dreams? As something they like to do?

They almost couldn't see the colors of the world around them, reducing all into a darker world where the sunglasses could only be taken off of their faces when they went to sleep.

In a cult of pessimism, where they believed they have the need to protect themselves from happy colors. From the happiness and joy they both longed and feared.

Such as their fear to love the perfection of their imperfect bodies.

The perfection of their individuality, with bodies made by measure for each one of them, always searching for a common ideal, nonexistent, utopic, where biometric measures put them under knives and diets, without to realize the beauty of their own beings. Hidden under so many layers of esthetic globalization.

Observing the persons, so similar inside, so different outside; spiritually identical, physically so different, Alessandra was thinking about things.

Was it so difficult to accept happiness in this world?

So difficult that persons always seem to search for the dark side of life? Why?

Too much brightness hurts their eyes?

Louis, the Geek, was content that his wireless system was perfect. He was content, but not really happy, something else was in his mind.

The Geek had a personal dream he was pursuing for years.

He wanted to find the members or, who knows, maybe even the founder, of probably the most secret society in the world: The White Angels.

The White Angels society was growing day after day; about that, the Geek was sure.

Walking among common persons, even their members usually knew only a few other members.

The Geek knew one of their rules: 2.5% from their profits went out of their bank accounts. Not always to the same account and also not on a regular basis. But when it did, it was mostly around 2.5% and the Geek was good with numbers.

For many years, he was following and searching accounts, trying to find them. He already had a list with possible members and his forensic evidence showed that they were probably growing.

But, who are the White Angels?

There was a rumor that the higher members shall have secret meetings and decide about the World's destiny. That some of the most important persons in the world belonged to them.

Inspired by the legend that in ancient times angels came to Earth to teach and help human beings, some persons believed that between the higher members, there shall be real angels, incarnated or not in human bodies.

There were lots of rumors about them, but the truth was that nobody seemed to know who they really were.

The Geek had already followed some of the persons in his list, to find out where the meetings were, but nothing came out of that. He couldn't just stop someone on the street and ask: 'Are you one of the White Angels? I've been watching your bank account for months and saw the 2.5% going out. Who are you?'

Because also, the accounts did not give enough links to follow the chain system. The money wasn't always transferred to the same account. And sometimes there was no transference at all.

The Geek also wanted to be part of the group.

He knew about them since childhood.

His parents were already not so young as he was born; he was an unexpected child that brought, together with his sister that came directly after him, happiness inside this old couple's life. They were not rich, and his father died, as he was still a child. There was a time, after his father's death, that his mother was worried, thinking about whether to take him out of school.

He should work and help at home, these were difficult times. But suddenly, after another day looking for a job, without finding it, she came back home and told him that he could stay at school.

She found a job shortly after this day, which allowed her to pay also for his university.

Asking her what happened, the only answer she could give him was that she had met a white angel. And things changed and she died years later, as an old woman, without explaining to him more about it.

To find the founder of the most secret of all secret societies was a goal that maybe not even the Geek could achieve.

But in searching for information about the White Angels, he found a strange communication.

It was best to contact his friend at the NSA, about the communication he found. There was a bomb, or more than one bomb, inside the Stadium. He needed to contact his friend, without speaking with the Council about it, to avoid more confusion.

He called Calvin.

Haidji

Chapter 27

Anthony rose early on the day the trial was to begin.

He had a coffee with Diana before the trial and told her about the Suicide Game, were he was hiding himself. He thought that Marcel, being her brother, had already told her, but he hadn't, he was a true friend. Even being a journalist, he could keep a secret.

Anthony told Diana because he wanted to impress her about his courage, and also to explain why he couldn't call her or answer her calls more than once or twice a day— there was no other woman. His wife did not count, he would divorce her after the trial, they already agreed about it, she wanted to marry her personal trainer and wanted kids with him, so better not to tell Diana the truth and scare her away.

Diana, of course, knew about his fake marriage. She was scared about the Game, so she asked Anthony to leave the game. He said that he would think about it.

Anthony, better AHG, was prepared. So was his legal team. The opening statements from both sides were expected to take more than two days. After that, the witnesses would be called. After the evidence was in, the closing arguments would take many days. Normal trial procedure. The trial was scheduled to last two months, at least.

AHG's legal team had a different plan.

Big Oil's case would be dismissed on a motion for summary judgment, to be made *in camera* in the presiding Judge's personal chambers, on the first day of the trial.

Before dressing, AHG had called his lead counsel. He asked about the trial preparation. They had completed their motions brief for the surprise summary judgment application. They had all the legal arguments written, with copies of all the relevant rules and cases. They had even included a summary of their surprise witness's evidence. Everything was ready to go. Any last minute polishing that might become necessary could be made on the fly, in real time, on their laptops in the courthouse. They could immediately deliver all their arguments to the Judge and his clerks, on thumb-drives.

For once, he was entirely satisfied with his conversation with his lead counsel.

'It's done. Let's roll.'

The courtroom was packed.

The clerk called the case, *Big Oil v. Gustav et al*, civil docket #53507-710-918.

The multiple attorneys for each side introduced themselves for the record, and it took a fair bit of time. 'Too many damn lawyers', muttered Judge Rubenstein to himself, so only his clerks could hear.

After the formalities, Judge Rubenstein started the trial: 'Counsel, are you ready to proceed?'

'We are, Your Honor', replied a chorus of legal voices, as would they be a choir of altar boys.

'Then let's proceed with the Opening Statements.'

'Your Honor, the Defense has a motion to be heard before the Opening Statements. It is a motion for summary dismissal of the Plaintiff's case, on the merits, and with prejudice. We respectfully submit this motion should be heard *in camera*, in your Chambers, for reasons we will explain when presenting our motion.'

Not knowing what was coming, the plaintiff's counsel objected to the *in camera* hearing, but without success.

'Counsel to my Chambers, along with the court reporter and my clerks', said the Judge.

Now safe from public view in his Chambers, and after hearing arguments on whether the Defense motion should proceed, Judge Rubenstein ruled in favor of hearing the motion. This way, he minimized the risk of a mistrial if the court of appeal ruled that the defense motion should have been heard. If either side lost anything in this case, the court of appeal was going to hear about it, that much was certain. The other thing that was certain in the Judge's mind was that he would do as much as he could to help Big Oil win.

'Your Honor, the foundation of our motion to dismiss is Big Oil's gross abuse of process in this case, including criminal conspiracy to subvert the course of justice. Before we cite you the relevant jurisprudence, you need to hear our evidence. And from that, you will understand why we have asked this motion to be heard *in camera*. Indeed, we think we are doing Big Oil a big favor, by proposing to do things this way.'

'Please proceed', said the Judge.

'We now call our first witness in this motion. Would the clerk please step outside and bring Mr. Louis Rousseau in; he is our first witness.'

The clerk brought Mr. Rousseau into the Judge's Chambers. After being duly sworn, the lead defense counsel examined him:

'Please state your full name for the record?'

'Louis Rousseau.'

'Do you have any nicknames?'

'In some circles, I am known as the Geek.'

'And your occupation, sir?'

'I am an information technology specialist.'

'And your work experience?'

'Most of my clients are confidential. It is generally known in my business that I have been on retainer to private corporations and advisory firms, and to certain US defense contractors, and also on occasion to other US government agencies; but, out of respect for the confidentiality obligations imposed on me, I should say no more than that.'

'And in the course of your work, have any such persons recently engaged you?'

'Yes.'

'And that is why you are here today?'

'Yes, as part of my work assisting a government agency in counter-terrorism, I was able to find and confirm a number of communications centered in and on the City. They emanated from the offices of Big Oil in the City or from persons otherwise established to be in the employ of Big Oil. Because these communications did not relate to terrorist activities, but rather, the private plans of a public US corporation, I was given clearance by the government agency to alert the intended victims, so they could protect themselves.'

'Thank you, sir. And, before we go through each and every one of those communications what, in summary, was the gist of them?'

'The communications established, beyond any reasonable doubt, that Big Oil was using illicit and illegal tactics to subvert the outcome of this trial including, but not limited to, threats made to the Judge and certain jurors to influence their behavior throughout the course of this trial. And also, a plot to kill Mr. Gustav, so he would be unable to testify in this case.'

'Preposterous!', shouted the Plaintiff's counsel. 'Your Honor, we object!'

But, the Judge knew better.

'Counsel, for the Plaintiff, I will give you 30 minutes to inform your client of this evidence, and to take instructions. We will resume in 30 minutes in my Chambers.'

Thirty minutes later, the Plaintiff's lead counsel stood before the Judge, in his Chambers. Reading aloud a proposed form of consent dismissal order. By consent, the case would be dismissed, on the merits, and with prejudice. The dismissal of the case would be made public in open court, as soon as everyone reassembled in the courtroom. By agreement of both sides, they would not reconvene in the public courtroom until after 4 o'clock local time, when the stock markets were closed.

Also, with the permission of both sides, the Judge would invoke provisions of the PATRIOT Act, so the transcript of the Geek's evidence would be classified, and therefore not available to the public.

AHG had won again.

6

After another coffee with Diana, AHG was back in the condominium. Confident and happy that if he could win this case...then, what was clear, he always wins...he could always win everything. He decided: he would not leave the Game.

ᕦ

Later that evening, AHG spoke with one of his Swiss bankers, who were calling from one of the bank's branch offices in the Caribbean to congratulate him on his win.

The banker confirmed that they had, that day, shorted Big Oil's stock, big time, on behalf of one of AHG's holding companies. They would cover the short position in the morning; the price was sure to fall on the news of the consent dismissal. AHG would be millions richer. He hoped the drop in the share price would be a big wake-up call for, or maybe even impose a conscience on, Big Oil's shareholders.

Also, he generously decided to give a million dollars to Red, just to make sure that he would win the Game.

Diana now understood that he wouldn't leave the Game, but she did not accept that. He asked her to come and watch the last days of it, but she refused.

His ambition had grown because of his fear to recognize his feelings for her. He wanted to prove how good he was.

Life is made by decisions.

We make decisions every day in our lives about almost everything around us. What we eat for breakfast, what we will wear, what way we will take.

Once a decision repeats, it turns into habit, and habits can become vicious; without to leave a note inside of your mind, they take the upper hand in your life and turn themselves into basic needs.

For AHG, to win turned into a basic need. He went back to the condominium, his stomach feeling strange. Turning as would it be inside a train. It was like to take a train and sit facing in the contrary direction. Like to go backwards in life. The train goes in the right direction. But if you take the wrong actions you fall backwards. Even then, the only sign that shows you that, is your stomach.

Like being on the right train, but sitting in the contrary direction, AHG entered the condominium. While Diana stood outside the condominium, paralyzed, looking across to the Stadium on the other side, seeing images of the candidates in their last jump, hanging outside the Stadium in their full 3D splendor; while the Stadium changed into the sky colors, as would the Stadium itself be invisible, and the candidates be hanging in the sky.

Haidji

Chapter 28

It was the day off, with many things to plan for the last game Step.

Alphabot opened the door and White, Yellow, Red, Green, Blue, Purple and Black entered the conference room. Sitting around the round table they agreed, without voting, that the wireless system to cut wires, tested the day before, was a complete success. It was so unexpected.

They watched images from the public's reactions and expressions in this last jump; this idea had brought the tension and adrenaline back into the Game. Nobody knew what would come next; persons were already renting helicopters, to watch the Game from the sky. Because there was no spot free inside the Stadium. Maybe also, to see the Windplate from the sky, and figure out how it works, in case of a new rainstorm.

The Gravedigger wondered what had happened, and blamed the storm and lightning for it. With only seven candidates, the Council didn't need him to take care of the gloves all night. They would explain that to him, and direct him to work as usher.

After the tempest, they needed more ushers to help with the dropped Candidates.

Purple suggested that models should dance on the last game Step. They can be transformed into a group of dancers, who dance to the Life in a Wire songs.

'We'll vote about it...now', said Black.

The Council voted, the answer was yes.

After the storm, only seven candidates were left. It was another day off. Purple suggested that they could give interviews.

'The Seven Last Candidates...Interviews? Reveal their names?' Asked Yellow.

'Let them speak?' Red was upset. 'Speak?'

'The Game would get boring; something need to be changed to make it more interesting', said Purple.

'The Game would get...boring', said Black.

And they voted again. Yes for the interviews.

Green voted against. But his vote wasn't the chosen one. 'Interviews? Are we here in a reality show? This is real life, my friends! Real life! And real death too! How can we know that they will jump? Did you all know that we will need to reduce the milk of amnesia dose, so that they can be able to speak? Do you really believe that they will jump just with all that neuro-linguistic programming and meditations crap?'

Yes, the other six council members voted. Yes, and yes again, they believed in neuro-linguistic programming. And in meditation. And six of them believed that all was always, at the end, in God's hands. Humans were children, on the hand of destiny.

But for one of them, God was always on his side. On the side of the same Council member, a member who practically chose himself. He touched his own metal sphere, 2.9 centimeters in diameter, one millimeter smaller than the other spheres. It was the only sphere that could pass through the bottom of the crystal ball. One millimeter was the difference between taking our own decisions in life, or letting it always be in the laps of the gods. The difference between being a child, or a responsible adult capable to take decisions and handle the consequences.

The laser projections were a success. They were all happy about it, should they show more to the outside public?

And they voted again, yes, let the outside public see more of what happens inside the Stadium.

Black, Purple, Blue, Green, Red, Yellow and White left the room and Alphabot came to close the door.

When the Gravedigger was directed to transfer to work as an usher, he was sad about it, at first. But then he was happy to leave, because after he started his usher work, he met an old contact from Spain who was at the Game, who got him a job, for after the Game. In a French cemetery, close to the Spanish border.

G

In the condominium, the seven candidates were taking their neuro-linguistic programming lessons and also, seminars about how to speak in public. They could prepare their own speech. This would make it more real, and bring them more confidence and will to jump and win the game. Models would be there to applaud after they spoke.

The Seven candidates moved into new rooms. But due to the fact that the staff of the game also used a similar uniform, it was as if the place would be full with candidates. All so that they didn't feel lost and lonely, before the last step of the game. But they had their meals now, inside their own rooms. To focus on the game.

Haidji

Chapter 29

Step 3 – Day 1

The crowd was there, waiting for the last seven candidates to appear, making their bets inside their minds, and in one or another case, inside their hearts too; choosing their preferred candidate, without to speak.

Every passing moment, the tension increased, more persons made their bets, more bought raffles; the more serious faces consulting their watches, waiting for the countdown to start.

Poker faces.

Also when it doesn't seem to be, time passes by. Minutes before the candidates were being prepared. Walking into the platform. Wearing their shiny black suits. With the orange shiny symbol on their foreheads.

The Hare Krishnas outside adopted the Life in a Wire melodies. They sold lighters again, no rain; together with the CDs, pre-loaded iPods, and songs.

Antipodes of the winners, the dead candidates would also be celebrated anyway. As a diamond on someone's finger, as a winning bet ticket in a bank account, or as a new organ inside a strange body. They would be part of the winners, from a certain point of view.

Their bracelets would be removed. His or her body sold, His or her belongings donated. Divided into pieces. And from the rest of his ashes, a diamond would be created.

No last meal. No last smoke. No last wish.

Luck, mixed by the hand of destiny, would decide their fate.

The air grew thick with the smoke of the public's thoughts. The applause for losers was as intense as for winners, in this suicide game. There were the diamonds.

Lots of diamonds, the night before, falling off of the platform.

The countenances of the candidates who remained turned more and more similar, after each jump; as would they be wearing poker faces, turning into players of the game.

In the silence between jumps, the only noise was that of bet sellers, walking with their pocket machines, counting and registering bitcoins. Like background music, as would the poker chips of death take the upper hand over the game.

Smoking was suddenly allowed in the Stadium.

The candidates' eyes were almost closing, exhausted, with all their muscles hurting from so much jumping. As would the game be more painful than death itself. And death would just be the expected trophy.

Like the moment in a poker game where someone is dealt the right or wrong card, and deals with the consequences.

Only one of them had the right card to win the game.

The tension increased, and the atmosphere was becoming almost violent inside the Stadium. The poker face was now showing the reverse side of the game.

Like in a poker game, all the others did not think about it. We all think that we can always be the one that wins. Can we? Independent of the rules of the game named life. Independent of our names or dreams. We all can be the one that wins. Only if we believe 100% in it, the problem is.

Only few persons really believe...100% in something.

This is something you know only...if you have the strength to keep going.

When the aching body stops because your mind doesn't feel it anymore...but you keep playing the game of life.

In the middle of the smoke of bad thoughts. In the middle of the bystanders of fear, in the middle of the night...a star shines over your dreams.

Restless and tired, with no break, waiting for the next card that can maybe never come, expecting the next move; so also inside the last step of the game, a departure is possible.

Luck takes unexpected ways sometimes; to decide who wins or who loses, and the poker face falls like a mask...over the sand on the ground.

$$\mathcal{G}$$

The Hostess recalled the last game day. After the storm, only seven candidates were left. She herself was scared that day. As she saw bodies falling all over the sandy ground, she thought that all candidates had died by reason of the storm.

Now, in front of the Stadium, fans of Life in a Wire were singing their hits, dancing the new dance. Suicide Freak choreography was the new hit.

The Hostess entered the platform through the elevator in the middle of the platform, in her Dolce&Gabbana red Femme Fatale dress and Alexander McQueen shoes, and announced:

'After the unexpected storm from yesterday, I want to introduce you to the third and last step of the Game.

From the 8000 candidates, we now have...Seven.

Yes, only seven survived the storm.

Falling with the raindrops of the storm, their souls must have been evaporated into the sky.

But now I have a Surprise for you.

You will see now, directly from the Night Stadium, to all Nations in the world.

For each one of you that has been here in the Stadium, since day one, suffering and celebrating with us.

And also for each one of you who switched on your TV, computer, or smartphone to follow the Game, and also for those of you who are inside the helicopters over the Stadium.

For each one of you that came to see and be with us, no matter when or how.

I will present a live interview, with our new Celebrities. Yes. They will be here today, in all newspapers, in all magazines, with their first, and in some cases also their only and last,

Live interview.

If you still have doubts about your preferred candidate.

If you still don't know to what side you should turn.

If you are new here, and want to know more before taking a decision.

I have now the honor to introduce to you.

The Ultimate Candidates.

Now

From the Night Stadium

For you

The Seven.

The spotlight fell over the seven candidates, standing on the middle of the platform.

One after one, they will speak to you

You will hear their voices

Know their names

And more about them

Here they are...

The Seven...the last step survivors from the Suicide Game

I introduce you to The Ultimate Candidates!

The light fell over the seven again, and then went dark, and the spotlight fell over the first candidate from the left.

'Candidate number 0907: Moma.'

And Moma spoke:

'We all look different, but we all are the same. We are all just human beings trying to make a difference in a world branded by globalization. We want to feel special; special, as we already are by birth special, special and unique; we are all the same under the banner of Life.

I am Moma, and I am here and you are there. I will jump and you will watch me, but we are together here in the Stadium, as we are together in Life and Death. Maybe I am one that dies, maybe I am the one that stays alive, but no matter what, we are together here and now. And we are all part of this game and responsible for every step of it. We are all equal. I can die, you can live, I can live and you can die one day, but no matter what happens here today, we are all the same, just human beings trying to be special, as we already are.'

There was applause for Moma.

The spot light went to the next Candidate.

'Candidate number 1518: Fabio!' Announced the Hostess.

Fabio's words were proud and angry:

'I've reached the final stages of this Game. I've risked my life, not yours, by entering the Game, only to discover that I entered this game already many years ago. I entered this game the day I was born in my beautiful village; I had no choice to choose, even when I thought I had it.

Bastards have overrun our society. Their drugs of choice are greed, blasphemy and sloth. Giving up my dream, entering what I thought to be a safe and clear business, I found out that not even water is pure anymore. You buy pure water and trash, plastic, burned oil, comes along even before you drink the first drop of it.

Indeed, nothing is pure—let alone sacred—anymore. No matter what you do, life seems to be just one long descent into hell. It does not matter anymore whether you are a sinner or a saint.

Haidji

I am a cyclist. An artist suffers because he must. But a cyclist suffers because he chooses to. The element of choice allows him to feel pleasure through the suffering, or maybe it is through the overcoming of suffering, that the pleasure comes, because even when a cyclist doesn't win the race, he wins, because he wins the battle against pain, again and again. For a cyclist, pain is pure and honest. You know the face of your friend and your enemy.

Pain is the only thing I ever found, that's really pure.

But now, due to the society I live in, I am a bike-less cyclist, descending into Hell, holding the wire of my life. Still in a race, with no bike. I am a bike-less cyclist.'

The Public sighed and breathed deeply for an instant...and then applauded for Fabio.

The spotlight went on to the next candidate.

'Number 3507.... Outside, he is Mr. AHG; in the game, he allows us to call him Anthony', announced the Hostess.

Anthony spoke clearly and calmly:

'I think that you must believe that you will win.

Because this makes your will.

Only your own will can do it, your will; and some connections can help you also, of course.

Practicing the bungee jumping here, I have learned how to fall, but most of all, I have learned how to stand up and celebrate the victory even before the next fall, because of connections.

Connections are almost all you need to win, even when you're brilliant like me. You need the right connections. Connections are the wires that keep you alive.'

After loud applause for Anthony, the spotlight moved to the next Candidate and the Hostess announced:

'Candidate number 4914: Jens Plaato.'

And Jens spoke:

'I don't need to introduce myself, everybody knows who I am.

I feel kind of depressed after jumping. Because I was not the first that died. But I can also be the first to be the last one. Or the first somewhere.

I get depressed when I am not the first, because I deserve to be the first, like you all deserve to have me on the top of your list.

We all deserve it. I see. I fix. I solve it. I deserve to win. Because I am me.

But you already know this. I am I. And you are here, with me, because you love me, and I love you for loving me. I love my image too. This is great. And I can be the first today, and you can be the first to bet on me.

Be with me. And I will feel you being with me here. Supporting my campaign. I see. I fix. I solve it. Thank you.'

Huge applause, for Jens.

G

The spotlight moved to Candidate 4918, Sarah Mondstein. After being announced, Sarah spoke:

'I did not know that I was a princess, living like a bad mistress, until someone told me. And I have won my own Kingdom, in three dates, only to lose the war against myself. And now all I want is to jump and forget about all that, because I can't live without a nameless man who found the way to my heart and updated all my dreams...'

Tim was distracted, but as she spoke, he recognized her in her words...it is really her...

'Don't Jump! Don't let her Jump!', he cried. Tim was paralyzed.

And Sarah finished her words,

'I don't know where this jump will bring me, but I hope that you are there, where I fall. Because no matter how deep I fall, no precipice can be so deep, like the deepness of the love I feel now, for this man who called me Princess... Will you be there when I fall? Is that were I will find you again?'

Silence. Some persons in the public had tears in their eyes. Nobody expected a love story.

The spotlight moved to the next...

Haidji

The Hostess announced:

'Candidate number 5151, Bianca White!'

And she said:

'He lived like a devil and died like a saint.

Life is paradoxical, but I believe that I could also be the person I am today, if life would have cut me with happiness, instead of pain.

I would be the same. I didn't need the pain to grow, or be who I really am inside of me.

Because life, life cuts you like a precious stone and shows the brilliance of your essence...but maybe we can learn also with joy and happiness, and turn into the same persons, just happier. We don't need pain to learn.

We don't need to suffer to grow. This is all a lie they tell us, so that we can accept all bad things in our lives, thinking that they make us to what we are. That is nonsense, because we are what we are, deep inside, since always, and our shine can also come to the surface, when we grow up with beautiful things, we don't need to suffer to grow. We can grow also through love and happiness.

Some days the world is no more or less than just a weird place.

Today is one of these days.

Ces't la vie, Carpe Diem, Veni Vidi Vici, Let's do it? Alea iacta est!!! ...No! It wasn't, and she laughed, it wasn't!!! It was I!!!

Let's jump into it!!! It's done! '

The public was speechless. Confused. As would the wrong person be standing on the platform.

G

The Hostess then announced the next candidate:

'Candidate number 7195: The Scientist.'

And The Scientist, a little bit shy, spoke:

'It is not that each one has their own truth, it is more that we see only part of it, and instead of waiting for the rest to appear, we build over optical illusions, and believe that this, Is! Instead of just contemplating the world around us and letting things speak, we answer immediately, before words enter inside our minds or hearts, or even souls. And this makes us believe in lies.

In the past, the Earth was like a piece of paper, and now planets have elliptical orbits. In the future, we will believe in other things that we cannot imagine now, and recognize the illusions and lies in our actual way of life.

Can the future be now? Are we prepared for it? I'm afraid we are not.'

Silence fell over the Stadium. As would the applause be coming from the soul of the crowd, instead of their hands.

The crowd, after hearing the Seven Candidates' speeches, bought more betting tickets. The diamond raffles were sold out. They could buy only betting tickets.

Alessandra did not have much money. But she decided, after hearing one of the candidates, to buy a bet ticket on him, not because she wanted to win, but because she wanted him to live and fulfill his dreams. She thought that maybe, who knows? Buying a bet ticket, for the candidate to survive, was like a sign to say. Don't let this person die.

6

The lights were off for a while, and then over all seven candidates again.

The counter started and the Hostess spoke:

'Now, there will not be only one jump. They will jump several times. And between their jumps, contests and concerts will be made. They will jump until death or exhaustion, welcome to the third and last step, welcome to,

SUICIDE GAME

The new game
The new mania
8000 candidates entered the game
Only one will survive
Only one can win! We have only 7 candidates left.
Live from the Night Stadium
Nothing compares to what you'll see here
Nothing compares to what you'll watch

You could hear their voices.

You know their names.
See, choose your candidate, bet
Participate! It is ...
The new and unexpected

... Suicide Game!!!!

Live from the Night Stadium
Nothing compares to what you'll see here
Nothing compares to what you'll watch
You have already chosen your candidate,

You have Made your bet

To be part of a

New and unexpected game

Now it's time to let all be in the laps of the gods

And to hear Life in a Wire, while the Seven Candidates
wait for the bell, to jump for their lives.

And when the bell rings...it is time to jump for your life.

But before that, we will have another surprise for you...

Haidji

Chapter 30

The Hostess spoke again:

'Welcome to the Third and last Step, welcome to

SUICIDE GAME

The new game
The new mania
8000 candidates entered the game
Only one will survive
Only one can win! We have only 7 candidates left.
Live from the Night Stadium
Nothing compares to what you'll see here
Nothing compares to what you'll watch

You could hear their voices,

You know their names.
See, choose your candidate, bet
Participate! It is ...
The new and unexpected

... Suicide Game

Live from the stadium of night
Nothing compares to what you'll see here
Nothing compares to what you'll watch
You have already chosen your candidate,

You have Made your bet.

To be part of a

New and unexpected game.

Now it's time to let all be in the laps of the gods.

And hear Life in a Wire while the Seven Candidates wait for the bell, to jump for their lives.'

And suddenly the counter stopped and the Hostess said:

'But before this happens, we will hear a new song from Life in a Wire.

Who are with us now...while the Ultimate Candidates wait to jump, here is Life in a Wire, with their new song.

A Kiss in Heaven.'

Tim was watching her every move. She was serene, graceful and beautiful on the platform.

He remembered something he once read, about patterns. Pattern recognition. He had seen it in a blog somewhere. Like Mark Twain once said that history doesn't repeat itself, but it rhymes.

But what if the current situation is very different. What if it doesn't rhyme with anything in the past? Even in this moment, he couldn't figure out how Sarah fit his rhyme. He had gone to Update to have sex. Now, he was in love with her. He could not remember his rhyme, his pattern. Maybe he never felt real love. Maybe he never had real sex. Why Update? Why Sarah? With her, sex was far more than sex, and love was asexual. He found asexual deep love, having great sex with her.

He would not let her go. If she died, part of him would die, too. He knew it. Felt it. Tried to explain it away, using his mind to control his thinking. He couldn't. Something more powerful than his thoughts. His soul had already made his decision for him.

Life in a Wire entered the platform, coming out the elevator in the middle of the platform, starting to play the slow opening chords of their new song.

'A Kiss in Heaven', announced the beautiful Hostess again.

The lights went out in the Stadium as the group started to sing, surrounded by the last seven candidates. Like statues facing the public. Shadows of the persons they were one day.

The melody started with the candidates moving like waves, and the models dancing like ballerinas around them.

The darkness took place of the space and I didn't notice.

Turning into black the mirror image, as the day became night.

Shadows gone from where they were hidden.

Looking for the sun that was already...gone.

The moment you arrive somewhere is the moment of Death

I want you on the Path. Don't wait at the end.

The moment you arrive somewhere is the moment of Death

I want you to be on the way, close to me.

Another day is gone and I'm still without you.

With the perfume of your presence inside my hands.

Inside my bones where you arrived as I tried to wash it out,

Made me smile, coming from the past into present time.

The moment you arrive somewhere is the moment of Death

I want you on the Path. Don't wait at the end of the street.

The moment you arrive somewhere is the moment of Death.

And not even know where the grave is, from my actual dreams.

Haidji

Another dark night came hiding the moon.

And I ask myself why...tomorrow, or yesterday, you didn't make me yours.

And painting starts in a kind of foreign country, you sent me the shine.

Hand painted your face for me, inside before a dark mirror space.

The moment you arrive somewhere is the moment of Death.

Grasp my hands; push me into you so long there is the Moon.

The moment you arrive somewhere is the moment of Death.

Can we jump at the end to the beginning of another street?

I fall asleep inside the star you painted for me.

Where the dark of the sky turned into blood red.

When a dream realizes, the idea dies.

Can you paint a blue star for us, a new one?

The moment you arrive somewhere is the moment of Death.

Can we fly, jump over crossroads, with lips painted by stolen cherry soup?

The moment you arrive somewhere is the moment of Death.

We cheat on time; smile between kisses and the way will never end

Be with me on the curves of the street.

Don't wait for me on the story's final point.

Grasp my hands, hold me next to you, and don't give me up.

Because our story can be a never-ending one.

The moment you arrive somewhere is the moment of Death.

And is there for the ones that left their dreams by their own luck.

The moment you arrive somewhere is the moment of Death.

Love that grows up, never stops and escapes the dark sword.

Don't tell me where you want to bring me, just take me with you.

Where steps are kisses and the path, an embrace.

Don't wait for me, take me with you.

Because the destiny is uncertain, while the way is already written.

And

If you forget all that,

And the black sword touches me,

Would you just bring me, A kiss in heaven?

Haidji

6

Silence fell over the crowd while the last words of the song reverberated throughout the Stadium.

The counter started to count down in silence, showing its shiny numbers on the screen.

The Hostess was herself speechless. Watching the candidates waiting to jump.

Tim stopped working and ran in the direction of the elevator, to go down to the Stadium ground. He fought with some Ushers on his way.

And he took the elevator, inside the platform structure.

The Council wanted to stop him, as they saw him through the cameras, but there was no time for the voting system. They started to discuss what to do, and did nothing else than discuss.

While Tim was in the elevator in the middle of the platform, coming up, the Hostess had regained her composure walking around the platform, saying:

'Welcome to

SUICIDE GAME!

The new game
The new mania
8000 candidates and
Only one will survive
Only one can win!
Live from the Night Stadium
The last 7 candidates are ready to jump
Nothing compares to what you'll see here
Nothing compares to what you'll watch
You already chose your candidate,

You have Made your bet

You have bought your raffle

To be part of this

New and unexpected game

Now it's time to let it all be in the laps of the gods

And when the bell rings...it is time to jump for your life!

10...9...8...7...6...5...4...3...2...1!

JUMP!'

As the countdown reached '5', Tim came out of the elevator.
Running over the platform, in Sarah's direction.

The Hostess tried to stop him. But the dancers were in her way. Tim embraced Sarah at the last second, and jumped with her. Kissing her.

Sarah's wire broke, and they fell together into the sand.

It wasn't possible to separate them.

They carried them away with one of the minivans.

There were more jumps this day. But nobody else died.

Only Sarah and Tim.

And in homage to them, Life in a Wire came back to the platform stage, to sing 'A Kiss in Heaven' again.

The crowd went out of the Stadium, crying.

It was a strong day. Worth the price of the tickets.

A real life Opera.

Haidji

Chapter 31

Part of the Geek's plea bargain involved 'community service'. But geeks, who hack into databases and compromise national security, don't usually get soup kitchen duty for their community service.

The Geek had to agree to allow the National Security Agency to tap into his talents. He would need to spend a stipulated number of hours per week on this, with tasks to be specified. His court record was dummied up with a counterfeit sentence, something like 'neighborhood soup kitchen for elderly persons in Precinct 78', just in case anyone checked.

It was because of this, that he called his friend Calvin, to speak about the bombs in the Stadium. It was his second call to Calvin, and Calvin seemed at first bored, because the first call, some days ago, was only about the Geek's information that it appeared a big company in the City was plotting to kill a key witness in an upcoming court case. Maybe even to kill a key witness. But the NSA wasn't interested in this. He should call only when he had something really important to share with them.

Now, he had found evidence of a planned attack on the Stadium. This was interesting. In a nutshell, the Geek explained to Calvin, the plot seems to be this.

There will be a terrorist attack; it will be an attack on the Stadium, during the Suicide Game. I am not yet sure how many people are involved, or the form of the attack. But for sure, the Stadium is the target, and the plans are already made. The communications I am seeing are commands; they are in execution mode now.

Calvin agreed this was something important, and compelling, for the NSA. They would put a team together and send them to the Stadium.

6

Michael was tired. Tired today, all month, all year. Michael was always tired.

Until now. Now he had a choice mission. He liked choice missions. They energized him.

His in-ear radio clicked and hissed with static, an incoming signal.

He heard Philip's voice, stuttering and stammering:

'H-h-hi, m-m-m-Michael, p-Philip here, wh-wh-ere are y-you n-n-now?'

'Goddammit Phil, you're talking to me, cut the damn stammer, will you? I can hear you fine. I am by the food outlet in Section C, watching people coming and going through Corridor C-2. Nothing so far.'

'Roger that. Talk again in 10 minutes, unless something comes up. Out'.

'Ciao'.

Michael said ciao because some people were walking by him. Philip must have been in a secure place in the Stadium, with nobody close. Philip was his CIA counterpart on this choice mission. As far as anybody who didn't have a certain top-level security clearance could tell, Philip was neither part of the military nor any similar agency. Nobody could finger him. No terrorist would ever suspect that Philip was a CIA agent, let alone one of their top assassins. Philip's perfectly unshaven, yet clean face and dark hair gave him a non-Waspish air. Perfect icing for the plainclothes cake. The cherry on the top was his own invention: his stammer, carefully cultivated, so people would think he was an idiot, an incompetent, a disabled schmuck; impotent, harmless.

Same for me, for that matter, Michael thought to himself. He was part of an FBI unit that didn't exist. Even in the records of the FBI. The only way a selected few people knew about him was by reputation. Dark reputation. In one of the very darkest of businesses.

Sure as shinola, Michael thought, whenever Philip was involved, it was going to be very interesting, maybe even exciting. Philip had laughed, telling him that he wanted to test his disguise, so he gave one of the Stadium security guards a bit of a mouthing off on entering the Stadium, just in case any terrorist was watching. The guard was taken in, and called for his supervisor, who then called Elisabeth. Elisabeth was the only other person who knew that some law enforcement agencies actually had agents in the stadium. But she did not know who they were, nor how many, nor their mission. She assumed it must have something to do with national security. Stadium security in particular. All part of normal protocol. Elisabeth made some new friends. She felt sorry for the one with the stammer.

The mission team had a third member.

Calvin, the NSA agent who had put the team together. Michael and Philip had worked together before, but neither had worked with Calvin. Calvin of the 'No Such Agency', Michael laughed to himself. In their mission briefing, Calvin gave the intelligence report based on the NSA's success in intercepting the terrorists' communications. Calvin was a key player in the NSA's long-running secret war on encryption using supercomputers, technical magic and what was politely known in the trade as 'human persuasion', to undermine the tools protecting the privacy of terrorist communications in the internet age.

Haidji

They liked each other from the beginning. They were true professionals. It was good for professionals to like each other. It was good for their mission.

Their mission, which did not officially exist: terminate, with extreme prejudice, any terrorist found in or around the Stadium. And any person suspected of helping such terrorist.

The Council did not know about that. Elisabeth didn't, either. They would tell them, when they found the terrorists; or maybe not, this was a command decision to make later on. When all was done.

6

It was a successful day. Even Red had tears. Unwanted ones; but tears in his eyes, as the public cried, seeing Tim jumping with Sarah.

They did not know the love story, but there was one.

Someone started to sell statues of a couple hanging on a life wire, in front of the Stadium; the makeup artist and the game candidate. As if he was falling in love with her while he was doing her makeup.

And fiction appeared, because nobody knew the real story, but it was love, and persons always want explanations for love things; it wasn't enough to feel it.

Sometimes the mind wants to be the heart, and the heart wants to think, and this create the fiction, for things we can't explain in a normal, common way.

Chapter 32

Step 3 – Day 2

The Hostess announced a new day.

After already jumping three times, none of the six remaining candidates had died.

The platform stopped at the height of the principal row of chairs, one more time, as she announced:

'Thank you for being here with me again. They will jump, until the wires break. It is unexpected, like life itself shall be. We don't know when a wire will break! But you all are here with me, after all these jumps. And I want to say, thank you for that.'

And she announced, one more time...

'SUICIDE GAME

The new game
The new mania
Six candidates left
Only one will survive
Only one can win!

Live from the Night Stadium
Nothing compares to what you'll see here
Nothing compares to what you'll watch
You have already chosen your candidate,

You have Made your bet

To be part of a

New and unexpected game

Now it's time to leave it all in the laps of the gods

And when the bell rings...it is time to jump...for your life!

10...9...8...7...6...5...4...3...2...1!

JUMP!

Fabio readied himself for the jump.

He thought of it as just another fast descent. No fear.

He glanced at the Hostess and made his flag by her colors;
green eyes, white makeup, red dress.

And then he jumped, along with the rest of the remaining
Ultimate Candidates.

Fabio was chasing his cousin Marco. Going faster than he ever thought he could go on a bike, down the descent of the Passo San Marco. Nothing held him back. Hurtling down the winding ribbon of mountain road, he rode straight through the rivulets of slippery water that oozed across the surface. Looking ahead, he saw Marco, also descending without fear. He let go of the brake levers completely. In an instant, he was flying. His front wheel almost touched the rear wheel of his cousin's bike. He knew he would catch him.

As Fabio passed Marco's bike, Marco handed him a pirate flag, as would he give him a bottle of drink, and then disappeared in the air in front of him. 'Now win...Fabio! For us! Win ! Ciao!'

6

The platform touched the ground of the Stadium. As the platform came up again there were some small spots on the Hostess's Femme Fatale red dress.

Some people looked up to the sky, to see if it was raining. If raindrops had somehow reached her. But the sky was clear. Another small spot appeared. They looked more closely. Tiny rivulets of tears ran down her face.

The Hostess quickly brushed them away with her hand.

She had never showed tears before. But she could swear that she saw a figure, like a transparent colored shadow. Going in circles around the winners. And a young voice, laughing softly. It was a little boy, riding his bike, holding a pirate flag and smiling. Pedaling around the winners, in circles around them and then around the platform. Like he had won some race, and wanted to make a victory lap. Was it an impression caused by the stadium lights, or a dream? Whatever it was, she saw it and this brought tears from her eyes.

Was she drinking too much champagne, celebrating with the winners? Or drunk from the game's atmosphere? She could swear that she saw a little boy with a bike and a pirate flag.

She put herself together for the next jump.

'The new game
The new mania
8000 candidates and only 5 left
Only one will survive
Only one can win!

Live from the Night Stadium
The last five candidates are ready to jump

Nothing compares to what you'll see here
Nothing compares to what you'll watch
You already chose your candidate,

You have Made your bet

You have bought your raffle

To be part of this

New and unexpected

Suicide Game'

With only five candidates left in the Game, the tension was huge. The game was coming to the end.

'Only one and a half days more, and we will know the winner. Have you made your bet?

The new game
The new mania
8000 candidates and
Only one will survive
Only one can win!

Live from the Night Stadium

The last five candidates are ready to jump
Nothing compares to what you'll see here
Nothing compares to what you'll watch
You already chose your candidate,

You have Made your bet

You already bought your raffle in the last step

As part of this

New and unexpected game

Now it's time to let it all be in the laps of the gods

And when the belt rings...it is time to jump for your life!

10...9...8...7...6...5...4...3...2...1!

JUMP!'

The five candidates jumped.

G

In front of all seven Council members, in the Command
Room, Morris touched the computer screen and a soft click
sound made an echo in his mind.

Jens saw a flash. As his wire broke. A flash of light, like from a camera. For sure it was a paparazzi, and he was falling. Seeing all his photos in magazines, backwards from the end to the beginning of his career.

Some persons say that when you die, you see your life from the end to beginning; Jens just saw his photos in magazines. From the last one, to the first one, he was always on the top of the list. Smiling about that, he died.

Haidji

Chapter 33

The terrorists were inside the Stadium, mixed in with the crowd. They were only seven in number, enjoying the game. The easiest way to catch them would be to find them inside the washrooms, at their prayer times. But of course, because they were searching for them with only the newest technology methods, the terrorists were safe.

They did not have contact with their leaders from the moment they entered the Stadium, day after day. All commands were given before, and all was done. The only thing they needed to do was to watch the game and stay among the crowd.

The NSA had contacted the other anti-terrorist agencies and formed the task force hit team to track and kill the Stadium terrorists before they could execute their attack. The Geek's hacking skills provided intelligence the team used to construct profiles, to enable identification of the terrorists and if possible, their remote leaders. The mandate of the task force had been summarized in three easy words: 'terminate, extreme, prejudice'.

They had asked the Geek if he could use facial recognition techniques, which, they said, would be more reliable than human perceptions and intelligence. There were security cameras outside the Stadium, at all entrances, and throughout the insides of the Stadium.

Like in modern city streets, the crowd had no privacy.

The Geek tapped into the latest software for an NSA crowd-scanning project called the Biometric Optical Surveillance System — or BOSS. The system was designed to help match faces in a crowd with names on the watch list — whether searching for terrorism suspects at high-profile events, looking for criminal fugitives in public places, or identifying card cheats in Las Vegas. They could even scan photos on Facebook and Twitter, to see if they got any hits. 'Problem is,' said the Geek, 'these terrorists have been instructed to apply makeup, like the rest of the crowd is now doing, to feel like they are part of the Game themselves'.

The task force's high-tech tools were being defeated by low-tech, primal human behavior. So, maybe they would need to rely on human intelligence. Of which there was absolutely none, in this particular situation. To find seven made-up terrorists in the middle of over 100,000 persons and avoid the attack, was like to ask an atheist to pray for a miracle; not impossible, but almost, because they forgot...the prayer times.

They really had no viable plan. To terminate the terrorists who were among the crowd.

Haidji

'Let's roll', radioed Calvin to Michael and Philip. 'Target three is heading towards the washroom. You implement on targets one and two'.

'Roger that', they replied.

The washroom was busy, with lineups. Perfect conditions. Calvin brushed by target three, jostling him gently to one side while reaching underneath his jacket and snatching something from his pocket, which he quickly put under his vest. He would examine it later. A terrorist left the washroom, passing close to them. But Calvin did not see him. Wasn't prayer time, the terrorist was just using the washroom for usual things. If they would have been there at Noon, they would have caught him.

Four agents arrived moments later with targets one and two. Calvin, Michael and Philip were already situated in the observation room for the interrogation room, looking into it through the one-way glass. Targets one and two were brought in and seated at the table.

Another agent told them he had bad news for them, sorry they had to hear it this way…and immediately both suspects' arms were tied behind their backs and handcuffed to the chairs. They were then searched. Each had a small plastic box. Each had a t-shirt with fresh orange color, the SG Game t-shirt. And their wallets, with the usual contents. That was it.

The items were taken into the observation room. Three CDs. They looked the same. Life in a Wire CDs. Their new album, containing some of the songs they would perform during their gigs in the Stadium.

The CDs were selling like hotcakes in the Stadium, at the official outlets. They looked more closely. These CDs did not have the holographic stamp borne by the original products. Copies. Counterfeits. Fakes. They examined the two t-shirts. Same deal. Copies. Fakes. Good ones, but counterfeits. No holographic labels.

Calvin took the item he put under his vest, taken from target three. He showed it to Michael and Philip. Another fake CD.

And that was all.

6

The team reported their findings to mission control.

They were very upset.

'What kind of lousy intel are we getting here?', screamed one of the commanding officers. 'I thought your source was impeccable. Here we are to chase and kill what is only a bunch of counterfeiters, nerds! What is this about a terrorist plot? Your intelligence is clearly wrong. Your intel guy, the Geek, is an idiot! He probably got the metadata all wrong, and the actual content of the calls too. Given all the legal wrangling in your country about NSA activities, he was probably more worried about whether he could justify a reasonable, articulable suspicion, than about the actual meaning of the communications. Sheesh!'

They decided to report something after this big confusion, to the Council. They reported that they caught the counterfeit mafia, due to an anonymous call made to them. The Council was happy about it. No words about terrorists.

And the seven terrorists were at their seats, always using the washroom at the same time, coming in or out of different washrooms, to their spots among the crowd inside the Stadium, waiting for a sign. Or waiting to die suddenly, with no sign.

Every time they needed to accomplish their obligation, they used the washroom for it and then went back to their places among the crowd...and waited for the next time they should pray.

Haidji

Chapter 34

Step 3 – Day 3

Yellow thought that they would exchange Moma on the last game day, against another man; that was the deal. If he doesn't die before, that is. That would be on the last game day.

But the terrorist attack wasn't scheduled for the last day. It was to be the day before. The terrorists knew that Moma had decided the attack should be the day before. It would be too high a price if they lost their specialist. They wouldn't exchange him against another man who would die in the game at the end of the last day. This was just an excuse they gave to Yellow, to avoid suspicion. Yellow did not know about any attack. He thought that it was just a kind of reckoning between political activists, training Moma to deal with his fears about acting in public. But the terrorists decided from beginning to say, in all their communications, that they would make the attack on the third day of the last game step, just in case any information would find its way into an uncertain place, and damage their intentions and plans.

Alphabot opened the door.

And brought coffee.

And asked Black about coffee.

'No coffee, no water...thanks', said Black.

Green spoke next.

All was going well in the game; no issues, no big problems.

They started to chat. The mood became lighter.

'Alphabot! Black doesn't drink coffee, or water. I wonder what he drinks? Maybe tea? You don't need to ask!'

Alphabot left in silence. And Blue said:

'He is being polite.'

'Alphabot is being...polite', said Black.

'How can he be polite?'

'He is a robot!' said Green. 'He is not being polite! He is just programed to ask, or not, depending on the command.'

Robots are robots, they don't know about feelings. They don't even think! They are not alive!

What do they know about life and death?

Haidji

And Red said:

'What do you know about death, Green? Since you were born, you never died, otherwise you wouldn't be here, complaining about all and nothing, all at the same time!' And he laughed.

Green became more upset. 'I am alive, but I can die any moment, while a robot...a robot never lives, and a robot never dies!'

Silence.

Black said:

'Death is when you are so broken...that nobody can repair you.

Not a mechanic...or a doctor.

Robots...die too.

Alphabot...is alive.'

Green responded:

'You are alive. I am alive. But Alphabot is a robot.'

Black answered:

'I am alive like...you.

I am alive like...Alphabot.

I am not an imitation of you. I am Alphabot's...friend.

I am Alphabot's...kind.

I am not a human imitation...I am...myself.

But now, I will...demonstrate what I said.

I will...die.'

Before the other council members could get out of their chairs, Black took his skin off his face, and showed the mechanism underneath.

Black was the newest model from the FACE team in Italy, which had also made the Personal Assistant for the Council's boss. Created by an Italian company, he could show human expressions, of course.

Black pressed a button under his toga, on the left side of his chest.

Suddenly Black fell down, crumpled over the round table.

Green started to cry, he liked Black.

'Can we repair him? Do robots believe in reincarnation?'

'Of course!' Blue said.

Green and all the others were in shock.

They requested Alphabot to come immediately.

Alphabot came. As Alphabot saw Black's face, without the human transgenic skin over it, he went out and came back with a glass of water.

In front of the Council Members, Alphabot made a motion, as would he drink the water. He dropped the water over his own robot face. Over his robot eyes.

With his self-made robot tears running down his face, Alphabot carried Black out of the room.

Purple, Blue, Green, Red, Yollow and White left the room, following Alphabot, to find a doctor...or a mechanic, who could give Black a new life.

The Hostess announced:

'Welcome to the third day of the Third Step. We have only four candidates. Four Ultimate Candidates. Only one will survive at the end of the game.

They will jump for you. For you here in the Stadium, for you that are watching from the streets around the Stadium, for you at home, at work, in the mob, or wherever you are! You are here with me.

Thanks for being here with me! We will have five jumps today. I hope that they all survive, for the last day tomorrow. But it is not my decision.

It is all...in the laps of the Gods.'

Moma, Bianca, Anthony and The Scientist were standing on the edge of the platform. The counter started at 50. 49...48...47...

The Hostess, wearing her beautiful red dress and her amazing shoes, announced:

'Welcome to the first jump of the third day in this Third and final step of the Game.

Here they are...

Moma! Bianca! Anthony! The Scientist!'

The spotlight felt over each one of them, as she said their names.

'The remaining cards of the suits in the deck of life, mixed by fate...

Welcome to you, welcome again to them.

Welcome to:

SUICIDE GAME

The new game

The new mania

8000 candidates started the game

Only one will survive

Only one can win!

Live from the Night Stadium

Nothing compares to what you'll see here

Nothing compares to what you'll watch

You have already chosen your candidate

Now there are only four Ultimate Candidates left.

You have Made your bet

To be part of a

New and unexpected game

Now it's time to leave it all in the laps of the gods

And when the bell rings...it is time to jump...for your life!

10...9...8...7...6...5...4...3...2...1!

JUMP!

Standing on the edge of the platform, in a half dream, Moma thought about his idea. He murmured to himself, '...peoples of any race or color—Arabs, Romans or Persians—are equal under the banner of God.

I promised to never kill someone, now I need to do it, to save the other ones... But I will pay the price for breaking my word. I am sorry'.

He jumped, together with Bianca, Anthony and The Scientist. But he touched his vest while he jumped.

Moma died immediately.

Morris saw it. The six council members were distracted. Morris knew that nobody was supposed to die in this first jump. Moma was hanging, dead on his wire. The platform descended several meters before the Council members saw that he was dead. They ordered Morris to take action. Morris touched the screen and cut Moma's wire. It broke only three meters from the Stadium ground. But he wouldn't survive; he was already dead.

As Moma jumped, he clicked the button on his vest. In the same moment, in seven different places in the Stadium among the crowd, seven different persons fell dead onto the floor. The crowd thought they fainted by reason of the game's adrenaline, but they were dead. Emergency responders came and took the bodies to the wardroom. No identification, no IDs. Nobody claimed their bodies. Demir would take care of them. Their bodies were burned inside, but maybe he could make a deal, and use them to make some diamonds.

ᘓ

Moma had changed the guts in the terrorists' suicide bomb vests. He made the same changes to his own vest.

From a traditional high explosive charge, detonated by a terrorist commander's wireless signal, to a strong electromagnetic field, triggered by Moma's own wireless signal. He engineered two wireless chips into the vest; one so the terrorist commander could see his signal connection, to know that all was going as planned. The second, to receive his signal.

He engineered the kill zone of each vest to be limited to one-tenth of a meter. The vest would kill its wearer, but not anyone more than 3.3 inches away from the vest's inner core. Anyone standing or sitting next to a terrorist would be fine, and would notice nothing.

The inner core comprised a compact energy storage device, a micro inverter and an electromagnetic field generator. The micro inverter transformed stored energy into a high voltage signal that powered the generator, which would, on command, send three silent and deadly pulses of electromagnetic radiation into the epicenter of the vest wearer's body. Sort of like a cigar smoker blowing out concentric smoke circles, but in reverse.

Their internal organs would be fried immediately. Cooked beyond any hope of redemption or afterlife.

Only three candidates remained.

The Hostess was about to announce another jump.

In the other jumps of this day, nobody died. And the Hostess announced that it wouldn't be only five jumps, they would jump until exhaustion.

Chapter 35

The Hostess said, in the way only she could:

'The countdown starts at 50...50 meters from here to the
ground of the Stadium, 50 meters...50 seconds for the jump,
50 meters to the ground, so...let the countdown start...You
are here with me, to see... the last 3 candidates.

You are here with me to see

SUICIDE GAME!

The new game
The new mania
8000 candidates and now only 3!
Only one will survive
Only one can win!
Live from the Night Stadium
Nothing compares to what you'll see here
Nothing compares to what you'll watch
You have already chosen your candidate,

You have Made your bet

To be part of a

New and unexpected game

And Now, it is time to leave it all in the laps of the gods.

Bianca, Anthony, The Scientist?

Who is the one that will win the game?

You have Made your bet

To be part of a

New and unexpected game

Now it is time to leave it all in the laps of the gods

And when the bell rings…it is time to jump…for your life!

10…9…8…7…6…5…4…3…2…1!

JUMP!'

The three candidates jumped. Nobody died.

The platform went down and up several times more.

And after their eleventh jump together, all three were still survivors.

The platform came up one time more, with the candidates and with Life in a Wire.

The Hostess announced:

'Let the countdown start again.

Bianca, Anthony, The Scientist…who will win?

Life in a Wire is here to play...while they jump! They will play while the candidates jump.

A round of applause, please, for Life in a Wire and their new song 'One way Road'. And a big round of applause, please, for the candidates!

Life in a Wire started to play as the countdown started.

6

Tired after so many ups and downs on the platform of life, Bianca drowned into her own silence.

The crowd, along with the whole public, cried now, by every one of their jumps. The public was emotional and out of themselves.

Only the three candidates remained in the Game. The public realized after watching so many jumps with no dead candidates—but only in the few seconds while they jumped—that they didn't want them to die.

Then they quickly forgot that feeling, taken by the adrenaline of the Game.

But for some small moments, the public realized...this:

Now that they knew their faces, their voices, and parts of their story...the candidates weren't just numbers and betting stubs.

Bianca was watching the public and hearing the Hostess' voice. Also, hearing Life in a Wire's song, as would the voice be inside of her, too.

'One way Road...One way Road

It's a one way road and I'm in the wrong direction

All comes over me, and I don't pay attention

It's a one-way road and I'm in the wrong direction

All comes over me, and I don't pay attention

And I say NO! To all could be and never was

And I say NO! To everything that hurts me

And I say NO! To the pain and past I have

And I say NO! You will never touch me again

It's a one-way road and I'm in the wrong direction

All comes over me, and I don't pay attention

It's a one-way road and I'm in the wrong direction

All comes over me, and I don't pay attention

And I say NO! To all my broken dreams

And I say NO! To the stupid world around me

And I say NO! To every day I cried

*And I say NO! Ces't la Vie! Carpe Diem! Veni Vidi Vici!
Alea iacta est ! Lets do it!'*

C

The Hostess announced:

'SUICIDE GAME!

The new game
The new mania
8000 candidates and now only 3!
Only one will survive
Only one can win!
Live from the Night Stadium
Nothing compares to what you'll see here
Nothing compares to what you'll watch
You have already chosen your candidate,

You have Made your bet

To be part of a

New and unexpected game

Now it's time to leave it all in the laps of the gods

And when the bell rings...it is time to jump...for your life!

10...9...8...7...6...5...4...3...2...1!

Bianca! Anthony! The Scientist!

JUMP!'

The three candidates jumped.

Bianca drowned herself inside the air.

Immune to the cries around her.

After a twenty-meter free fall, in front of six council members, Morris touched the computer screen in the command room.

And Bianca's wire broke.

The public screamed.

But Bianca, Bianca was immune to their cries.

Immune to her own pain, she saw a starry sky opening in front of her.

It was her turn.

Her turn to be drawn inside the air and find the peace.

Falling off the platform of life.

Falling into a starry sky...crying, and falling.

As her body touched the stadium ground, she died.

6

The platform went down slowly, with the two last candidates hanging from it.

And then up again, with the two last candidates celebrating.

The public was amazed. Their adrenaline levels very high. They needed a Suicide Dog before they left the Stadium.

And the Hostess declared the end of this Third day of the last Game step.

Haidji

Chapter 36

Step 3 – Day 4

The Hostess announced the last day of the Game.

'Welcome again to the Stadium of Night, to the last day of this amazing game.

We have now only two candidates: Anthony, and The Scientist! Who will win the game?

Special thanks for you that have been here with me for many days, here in the Stadium, and at home, at your work places or even in the shopping centers, or helicopters, or walking the street...thanks for being here with me.

Here they are, for their first jump in this last day:

The Scientist! Anthony!'

The spotlight fell over the two last Game Candidates.

'With no delay, the countdown is starting...welcome to

SUICIDE GAME!

The new game
The new mania
8000 candidates and now only 2!
Only one will survive
Only one can win!

Live from the Night Stadium
Nothing compares to what you'll see here
Nothing compares to what you'll watch
You have already chosen your candidate

You have Made your bet

To be part of a

New and unexpected game

Now it's time to leave it all in the laps of the gods

And when the bell rings...it is time to jump...for your life!

10...9...8...7...6...5...4...3...2...1!

JUMP!'

Anthony and The Scientist jumped.

They jumped two more times before lunchtime, and did not die.

The crowd took a break to eat some suicide dogs, wondering if one of them would die today; they were both tough souls.

After a few jumps more, the sun was almost going down over the Stadium.

The Hare Krishnas were selling lighters again. The crowd used them like candles, for the now still alive, for one of the two candidates, for the last candidate to drop out the game. R.I.P., but rest, finally, was what the crowd was saying, speaking with the voice of their lighters' flame.

6

Alessandra was with Dawn, Wow, Cassandra and John, watching the jumps of the day. Already habituated to the game atmosphere, she left the baby close by, playing with Wow, around her.

With no body to bring up, Demir himself took the elevator to the street floor. He wanted to buy a suicide dog. What a game! He was happy with the results. He had forgotten to wash his hands, which smelled of blood, as would blood be his own private perfume. In a reflex, he cleaned his hands with an old cloth, which he threw on the elevator floor.

Wow smelled blood as the elevator door opened, and started to go in the direction of the elevator.

Demir saw the dog; a suicide dog, what is he doing here inside the stadium? Who brings a dog into a game like this? In the rush to go out of the elevator to buy his own suicide dog, he did not see Dawn following the dog into the elevator. The baby went quickly inside and the elevator went down.

Alessandra was chatting with Cassandra and the others, and had not seen Dawn walking away, following Wow.

6

The dog went out of the elevator and started to walk around, sniffing the gray sand.

Dawn saw the Hostess in her beautiful Femme Fatale red dress and Alexander McQueen red shoes, and followed her onto the platform.

Between the Hostess, the models all dressed in blue, the champagne glasses, Life in a Wire, and the two last candidates...nobody noticed Dawn crawling onto the platform.

The platform stopped at the height of the principal row of chairs, 51 meters from the Stadium ground.

The Hostess announced:

'Now, here, especially for you, after this long last day, is our favorite band, Life in a Wire, performing a new song, with only two candidates left...in homage to all who have died in the Game.

Life in a Wire, alone on the platform, will sing for you, a new song! And the candidates will come later, to jump for you, until only one of them survives.'

Life in a Wire began to play and sing. Softly.

Death on Death

I say good-bye
You'll watch me die
Will I be dying too?
Deep inside of you?

You say good-bye
And you think you'll be free
But I'll be awaiting you
In your final destiny

Because death on death

Is our favorite color

Death on death

Is our only mystery

Death on death

Is a powerful drug

And Death on death

Is the only way to be

We all say goodbye

And we all want to die

'Cause our peace it never lasts

And our life goes by so fast

Because death on death

Is our favorite color

Death on death

Is our only mystery

Death on death

Is a powerful drug

And Death on death

Is the only way to be

Haidji

Does anyone ask why
Does anyone even try?
If all we can do is cry
Then we should all want to die

Death on death ... favorite color
Death on death ... only mystery
Death on death ... final destiny
Death on death ... is alive inside of me.

Nobody had just died, but tears were flowing everywhere now.

Only two candidates remained.

They were on the platform, getting ready to jump.

Anthony was thinking about Diana.

He was busy winning everything and lost...her.

Because.

Happiness is just a dream.

A death dream that I lived with.

To be happy, without myself trying to be happy without you.

Because you and me were two, too strong, forces together.

An explosive love that, only when separated, survives our passion.

Maybe I was just afraid of the explosion.

But invisible, you're still there.

And now I know that I will not survive without you.

And when I die, you will die too.

Because I couldn't see that only together with you, and not apart, could I keep the pureness in my life. And love. Love.

Love always wins, love was my winning card, but I lost it when I decided to stay in the Game.

Haidji

The voice of the Hostess rang out, awakening the crowd from their melancholic mood, like an alarm clock:

'It's time for a new jump. Will this be the last one?

Are you ready for it? We are all anxious. You, me, Anthony, and The Scientist!

Without further delay, let the countdown begin.

Welcome to what might be the last jump, welcome to...

SUICIDE GAME!

The new game
The new mania
8000 candidates and now only 2!
Only one will survive
Only one can win!

Live from the Night Stadium
Nothing compares to what you'll see here
Nothing compares to what you'll watch
You have already chosen your candidate

You have Made your bet

To be part of a

New and unexpected game

Now it's time to leave it all in the laps of the gods

And when the bell rings...it is time to jump...for your life!

10...9...8...7...6...5...4...3...2...1!

JUMP!'

Anthony saw the baby walking to the edge of the platform. He looked closely, as the baby embraced the Scientist's legs and the Scientist, in an automatic reflex, took the baby up in his arms.

Just moments before jumping, Anthony realized that he would not survive the game.

As he realized this, he saw among all the persons in the crowd, a person dressed in white, the only person in white, in the middle of the Stadium audience. The cameras focused on her figure. Nobody understood why a woman dressed in white was there, cold and quiet like a statue. She was standing there, while a tear fell from her left eye, running down her face.

It was Diana.

Before he jumped, he saw Diana clearly.

Anthony looked to his side, and saw the baby still in the Scientist's arms. Without words, he made a sign.

He knew the decision that the Council needed to make.

As the counter showed the number 5, he pointed to himself and then made his finger down. Then he pointed to the Scientist and the baby and pointed his finger up, and nodded his head, as if he would be saying...it's ok.

In the control room, Morris got an urgent message to change the program for the jump in the computer. Could be done with a single touch. The wireless way to cut wires was perfect and fast. This all happened in seconds, before the jump.

In front of Alphabot and the seven Council members, with Black now in his new life without any transgenic skin, Morris touched the screen.

The Scientist jumped, seemingly kind of away from there, holding the baby in his arms, thinking about how beautiful jumping was.

And Anthony jumped. Seeing Diana's image in the crowd and on the screens. He closed his eyes to keep her image in his soul.

The public was speechless.

6

Diana had seen Anthony's sign and understood his message. She knew that he had paid to win. And she saw what he did.

She cried and went through the crowd, searching for the elevator to go down. They would not have his body. He had already paid too high a price for his jumping experience. Higher than even he had expected it to be. He deserved to win. Diana realized that real love touched his ambitious heart.

Alessandra had seen the baby's image on the screen, and ran as fast as she could towards the elevator, to go down.

Both women had gone towards the elevator together, while the bodies were falling.

Both worried about persons they love.

The Hostess had tried to run onto the platform to take the baby away from the Scientist's arms. Almost falling with her high heels.

But it was too late. They jumped already.

After falling...the atmosphere in the Stadium went misty with dry ice again. Silence overtook the crowd, while a song started to play, at first very slow and low, to the drumbeat of a funereal march.

We all gonna die
Someday
Some way
We all gonna die
Someway
Someday

One day on the subway
A man comes with a gun
He shots for your money
And then you're really done
                    And we all say goodbye

We all gonna die
Someday

Someway

We all gonna die

Someway

Someday

One day on the beach

You wanna make a swim

But a shark comes too fast

And in peace you need to rest

      And we all say good-bye

We all gonna die

Some day

Some way

We all gonna die

Some way

Some day

Don't wait for the day

Take your life, make your way

Jump into your destiny

And be part of history

      And we all say good-bye

We all gonna die

      Haidji

Some day

Some way

We all gonna die

Some way

Some day

No matter how you die

Or what action you take

Since you're born

Life is just a Suicide Game...

The platform started to come up, in the middle of the misty atmosphere. The Stadium lights were still diffuse. Suddenly the music started to play faster, louder; the vocals coming through more, 'Since you're born, life is just a suicide game...'

Spotlights fell over the platform. The Hostess stood there, wearing her red Femme Fatale dress. In a circle, models all dressed in blue were dancing, as would they be petals of a big flower, hiding whatever was in the middle.

Circles and circles of models in blue, coming from the middle, to the edge, of the platform. Once closer to the edge, they sat on the floor. The lights went completely off. And then, on came a single spotlight.

In the middle of the platform...was...

The Scientist. With a new spark in his eyes. Holding Dawn in his arms.

The public stood up to applaud. Tears were in each person's eyes.

The Hostess didn't need to speak. But she would say good-bye.

Diana was on the ground, next to Anthony's body. She covered him with her white scarf. No usher would carry his body away. No diamond would be made. They could give a fake one to the winner. She would, herself, spread his ashes over the sea.

Alessandra was worried about the baby. She didn't even realize that she had, along with another hundred persons, won the bet. It was more than enough money to live in peace for the rest of her life. Only one hundred persons had bought the Scientist ticket. But for now, she did not realize that.

She was happy as she saw Dawn on the screen, in the Scientist's arms. Happy and alive.

Even if she was only twenty years old, the last moments, more than all the days together in which she was more like an older sister, had turned her into Dawn's mother. She embraced Wow, who was also in the ground of the Stadium. Yes, they were her family...Dawn and Wow.

On the platform was the real diamond. Waiting for the raffle winner.

The winner of the diamond came to the platform, to shake the Scientist's hand. The signed poster would be sent to his home address later.

The Hostess said good-bye.

The models said good-bye.

The Scientist himself said good-bye, but in a kind of faraway manner, because the milk of amnesia was still in his system.

And Dawn said softly, 'hi'.

Dawn said 'hi' again, this time looking at the Scientist, smiling safely in his arms.

And then, from the Scientist's arms, Dawn looked straight ahead, and said, 'Hello'. And smiled.

This was the last image, and sound, from the Suicide Game.

The Game's last image and sound was frozen on all the screens, inside and outside the Stadium and on every mobile and fixed device.

The crowd started to leave the Stadium, and then the streets around it.

The night covered the City like a blanket. Not a blanket like some persons might imagine, but a blanket with infinite small holes, to let the star shine come through and bring new dreams to the Earth's surface.

No, the stars are part of the blanket, the part that brings the warmness we need to sleep in peace. Like dreams, the stars are part of our reality, and are part of us.

The shiny part.

Sometimes your dream is stronger than you are yourself. And life finds a way to keep it alive.

Sometimes your dream is so special that...you can't kill it. You can't die, even if you try. Life will find a way to fulfill it, and a way to keep you alive.

Because the Earth...the Earth needs dreamers...to survive.

Haidji

Haidji

The opposite of death isn't life

it's Birth

When you die

You just move on to live

Somewhere else

So painful it is

Sometimes a Dream must die inside of you

A Dream that never had a chance to be born

Under a starry sky

Beyond a sunny day

You pray and recognize

That maybe wasn't a dream

But just a nightmare

That almost killed you

Before a good dream could rise in your life.

Haidji

Haidji

About the Author

Artist, painter, writer, designer, photographer, performer. Just...Haidji.

Her interest in art began at the age of four when she got a blackboard for Christmas. She then started to draw objects around the house: chairs, tables, and so on. As she was twelve, she started to write her stories and poems. Handwritten and hand-painted books, for family and friends.

Her University education was at the University of Applied Science at Idar-Oberstein, Germany, where she obtained a Diploma (equivalent to a Master's Degree) in Jewelry and Precious Stones Design, and Painting. She is also a qualified and awarding-winning Goldsmith.

Haidji is a talented and creative artist who produces abstract work that resonates with warmth and life. Her stories create images in the reader's mind, as would a word be a brushstroke painting inside your imagination. There is a very spiritual feel to her work, almost an otherworldliness. A captiving blend of Brazilian flair, Teutonic precision and Dutch pragmatism makes Haidji's work unique, appealing and thought-provoking.

Since 1995 Haidji has exhibited her work, realised her projects and told her stories in many countries: Germany, Brazil, Italy, The Netherlands, Switzerland, England, Portugal, Spain, South Africa, Australia, and the United States of America.

A personal note from Haidji, for her readers:

Thank you very much for reading my book.
If you enjoyed the book, please consider leaving an online review, even if it's only a line or two; it would make all the difference and would be very much appreciated.

Best wishes, Haidji

Contacts:

Blog – www.haidji.blogspot.com

Email – haidji@gmail.com

Facebook official page – Haidji

Twitter – Haidji

Haidji